More praise for

White Swan, Black Swan

"These lovely stories about ballet are themselves balletic. Adrienne Sharp's choreography is first-rate."
—JOHN BARTH
Author of *The Sot-Weed Factor*
and *The End of the Road*

"[A] bold debut . . . For the characters here, who include fictional-ized versions of Nureyev, Baryshnikov, and other ballet stars, life rushes forth onstage, in movement, in the great romantic *ballon* of the ballets themselves. . . . [Sharp's] subject matter is, well, addictive, and universal in reach."
—*Elle*

"Reading Sharp's stories is like watching a magnificent ballet and then getting to go backstage and sneak straight into the dressing rooms, invisible. This book is a full theatrical experience, complete with demigod dancers and life-threatening passion, alongside ab-solute and terrifying human frailty."
—AIMEE BENDER
Author of *The Girl in the Flammable Skirt*

"Remarkably assured debut collection of interconnected short sto-ries that animate the passions and jealousies, the shining moments of beauty and shadowy pains, the evanescent highs and the lingering longueurs of the dancing life."
—*The San Diego Union-Tribune*

"In elegant prose, Sharp explores the world of ballet and its fringes, unafraid to look boldly beyond its beauty into darker aspects. This is a stellar debut."
—JOHN RECHY
Author of *City of Night*

Please turn the page for more reviews. . . .

White Swan,

Black Swan

Stories

A D R I E N N E   S H A R P

Ballantine Books • New York

for Todd

Acknowledgments

I would like to thank Gina Nahai, Marilyn Stachenfeld, Sandra Tsing Loh, Teresa Yunker, Dawn Newton, Debra Tratt, Mel Miles, and Laraine Crampton for their reading and rereading of this book. Thanks also to my editor, Courtney Hodell, her associate, Tim Farrell, and my agent, Sandra Dijkstra, for their commitment and belief. And to my parents, much love and gratitude.

Contents

Contents

Author's Note

This is a work of fiction. While George Balanchine, Suzanne Farrell, Tanaquil Le Clerq, Rudolf Nureyev, Margot Fonteyn, Alexander Godunov, Mikhail Baryshnikov, Frederick Ashton, and other people who actually lived or are living appear in this book as characters, my rendering of their lives is my own. In those stories where actual incidents involving well-known dancers and historical figures are described, I have made some changes in locale or costume for dramatic purposes, and I have taken the liberty of inventing some private moments for these characters. Some of the characters' remarks have been taken from interviews, though most are fictitious. Other than these characters or other well-known dance personalities who make brief appearances for reasons of verisimilitude, the characters in this collection, their interactions, dialogues, and situations, are entirely products of my imagination and are not intended to depict any actual people or events.

Bugaku

I've got a heating pad on my knee, an ice pack on my ankle, and I'm smoking a cigarette, which I shouldn't be doing, but Ridley's making me nervous. He's dancing tonight, not me, but that's not what's on his mind. He wants to talk. He wants to talk about turning thirty last week in Chicago, about moving to a bigger apartment when we get back to New York after the tour, about buying furniture, or at least a sofa, about getting married, about having a baby. Even though I've been with Ridley for four years now, ever since I was fifteen, none of this has ever come up. Dancers don't do those kinds of things. You're at the studio by ten, home from the theater after midnight: there's no energy for anything else. And a baby? That's at least a year off, if you ever make it back. But I don't want to fight with Ridley: I wouldn't want him to fight with me two hours before *my* curtain. So right now, I'm smoking a cigarette and trying to ignore all this.

"Don't answer me, Joanna," Ridley says from his side of the bed. "Try something new."

He disappears into the bathroom, abandoning me to this hotel room: a triple bureau and a writing desk, two wide beds with obelisks for headboards, a wing chair. Maybe this is what got him started. Nothing wrong with a good hotel room. I just don't see why we have to have all this stuff at home. We pretty much live at the theater; our apartment is only a warehouse for laundry and mail. I put out my cigarette, which was actually from Ridley's pack—we alternate, swearing off tobacco—and go back to what I was doing before he came out of the shower: going through my theater trunk. I've got about thirty pairs of pointe shoes dumped all over the bed, some white, some pink, some with the shanks ripped out, some I've used for two ballets but still can't bear to part with. I find the white shoes I need for *Bugaku* tomorrow night, for my first really big role—it's just me and Nilas out there on the stage for the whole adagio—and then Ridley's out of the bathroom again. I creep over to the door with my white shoes and silently stick the tips of them into the doorjamb, crunch the door closed. I've got to break the shoes in.

"Do you have to do that now?" Ridley says.

I turn to look at him, shoes on my hands. Without saying another word, he gets his bag and then opens the door to the hall and slams it behind him.

In about twenty minutes I'll go to the theater to watch him dance.

He's doing "Rubies," Eddie Villella's old role in *Jewels*. I'll be dancing Suzanne Farrell's role in "Diamonds" winter season back in New York. We're constantly replacing each other, but we never really own the roles. What Balanchine made for Farrell or Villella will always be theirs. To me Ridley looks like a young Eddie Villella, with that same robust energy and muscular attack. He's already on with Molly by the time I get to the wings in my leather jacket and twenty bracelets—I keep expecting there will be cabs all over the streets in L.A.—and I have to hold my hands over my forearms to keep the jangling muted as the two of them speed through the slapstick contortions that mark the opening movement. Molly has her hair wound into a cone that sits on her head like a pointed horn Ridley has to dodge, and her legs are astonishingly strong and knotted with muscles, almost the legs of a runner. But it's Ridley who does the running, peeling away from her for that wonderful, unexpected lap around the stage. Molly holds out her hand when he returns to her. Ridley slept with her once, when we were first going out, when he couldn't believe he was considering an affair with a child and felt compelled to make an effort to be with a woman his own age.

Ridley was already a principal dancer then, and I was just out of the School of American Ballet, earning $175 a week in the corps. I was prepared to adore him from afar forever when I was picked to rehearse *Firebird* with him; they always use a young girl for that, young and fast. But I turned out not to be that type of dancer, not fast enough, not vibrant enough. Management didn't like the way I looked with Ridley, either, and to this day I'm still being cast with Nilas Martins, who's more of a Jacques d'Amboise type.

But Ridley and I came together anyway. The baby and the star. I can't even imagine being in the company and not being with him. He's taken care of me, practically brought me up. When my parents and my brother James come to New York, it's like, who are these people, they can't help me, nothing they know is of any use to me. Ridley's the one who got me out of the corps, who tells me what to say when my contract's negotiated, who still coaches me in all my roles. He's the one who showed me how I lost out on *Firebird* because I wasn't concentrating hard enough, because I didn't block out everything but the image of that wild, jeweled bird so that when I moved I was nothing but hollow bones, feathers, and air. Ridley's the reason I just signed this season as a principal dancer. He's the reason I'm starting to make it. Dancing and Ridley: synonymous. Or, anyway, used to be.

Molly pitches herself into the wings at the end of their variation and collapses in a parody of exhaustion, does a free fall onto her back, a red angel in the snow, but there's no snow here, it's hard floor she falls on. She heaves spastically, going, "Oh God, I can't do this," but of course she can, she does it night after night. I watch her as she tries noisily to recover her breath, and I think, Why am I standing here holding my bracelets? as she goes on gasping, twenty decibels above the orchestra, while Ridley begins his solo. His skin is pale beneath the crossed straps and wide armholes of his jeweled costume, but his face is jubilant. His solo is half tongue-in-cheek, half big bravura, and I watch the way he flirts with the audience on a slow cross step and then vaults into the air away from them—theirs for only a moment. I grip the black canvas folds of one of the wings.

Beside me Molly slowly recovers, but not too slowly, she has only two minutes, and she begins doing the kind of repair work you do in the wings, ribbons, hair, straps, and then we're both standing there, side by side, watching Ridley. She whispers, "Do it, do it." She's there with him in a way I can never be. I'd trade places with her in a minute—just let me dance with Ridley, she can sleep with him.

Okay, maybe that's an exaggeration.

But I am jealous, really jealous of the absolute knowledge she has of his body. He's so beautiful, truly soulful, when he's moving;

he has an absurd kinetic confidence that lets him skim cream through any role, his body magically and alternately built for speed and gyration, elongated for purposes of carriage and line. He's like a god out there in that white light.

Outside Ridley's dressing room it's the usual pandemonium of delirium and relief, girls running around in tights saturated a translucent pink, their hair equally wet, yelling about how the tempo was off or watch out for that one part of the stage that was so slick. I can smell them from here, that heady, familiar mix of perfume, hair spray, he-man stink, and resin, which rises like a grainy mass and follows us everywhere. Other girls in their white "Diamonds" costumes for Act III of *Jewels* warm up, sweaters and Baggies masking until the last minute their scooped out, spindly legged profiles. Ridley comes in, a towel twisted around his neck and the legs of his tights pocked and streaked with what-ever black stuff Molly scruffed up off the stage and spattered onto him. His hair is greased into a multitude of tiny pointed spikes, something Balanchine probably never would have allowed, even though he let us girls do any outrageous thing we wanted as long as it made us magnificent.

"Joanna," he says, and he shuts the door behind him, sticks his hands inside my leather jacket, which is his, and I have that moment I often have where I can't believe Ridley belongs to me. He's got me up on the dressing table, backed against the mirrors into which he's wedged his talismans: various photographs of us, of his best friend Don, who retired last year, of Rudolf Nureyev, of Erik Bruhn. I've stuck a Polaroid up there, too, of Ridley blowing out the candles on the cake we brought onto the stage last week, his face miserable above the strip of flame. He's not miserable now, though, he's luminous and wet, face orange and beige, the black lines around his eyes unraveling into a blur.

"I was good, wasn't I, Joanna?" Ridley says. "I was very, very good." His tongue is thick in my mouth, swollen and bizarre from his exertions, and he's unwrapping my clothes, and then his, which are sticky and all coiled inside each other, his jeweled top, then his tights, and the cup he's started wearing when he partners Molly. Ridley's saying, "Talk to me, Joanna," until I say, Yes, you were very, very good, and then he barks and growls, licks at what he can reach until I can smell my skin coming off his breath. We're always like this after a performance.

The first time we made love was in Ridley's dressing room at the theater. We'd just finished *Nutcracker* and I'd knocked on his door with a Christmas present for him—a gold tie clip I had taken an absurd amount of time to choose, especially since Ridley didn't own any ties. I was nervous. My hair was down, still clouded with grit and the odd fleck of paper snow. Or what passed for snow after a month of *Nutcracker*s, with the stage-hands sweeping the flakes up off the filthy stage for the twenty-ninth time and dumping them on us for the thirtieth. Ridley pulled open the blue ribbon on my present, and then he pulled some speck from my hair, and then we were touching each other, Ridley going, "I don't believe I'm gonna do this to you, Joanna, have you ever done this before?" and I was afraid even to shake my head no, afraid he might stop what he was doing. Now Ridley's going, "Tell me you'll marry me, Joanna." He makes me cling to him while he parades me about the small room, holding my mouth to his, his hands under my thighs, his body the axis around which all other objects rotate and blur. I've got my head back and I'm almost saying yes, and then I catch a glimpse of myself in the mirror, a woman in street clothes hanging on to a man in costume, and that's exactly what I'm afraid of.

We're at Cocola, a place one of the local stage managers told us about. Ridley and I don't usually do this kind of thing—we're always too tired, or our schedules are too tough, but here at the end of the tour, we figure what the hell. Ridley's given his last performance, mine's tomorrow night, and it's the kind of mode where you want to change your life, or think you can. The cab ejects us at a long, narrow nightspot that stands practically alone in the eerily bombed-out landscape. Tiny tables are linked like train cars at one side of the room, a thin bar rolls down the other, and a three-piece band plays, valiantly, scrunched up at the deep back end Ridley and I tango toward.

We can see ourselves in the mirrored walls on both sides, which only adds to our pleasure in each other. Ridley's dressed like Mr. Clean—white pants, white boots, white sweatshirt, and I've got on a long black dress, one of those Lycra things that's almost like dancewear. Neither of us can keep from looking at our black and white reflections, but we look without shame or self-consciousness. Onstage we have to do it for others without the comfort of the mirror, but here we can have it both ways: draw a stir from the crowd and check on things at the same time. By the end of our first number we've attracted a fan other than ourselves, or Ridley has, anyway. It's a woman, who asks him to dance. Not in the choreographed script, but Ridley is flattered and intrigued, I can see that, the whole of Cocola can see it, and the three of us just stand there for a moment, the woman absolutely self-possessed, until finally I break our frieze and sit at the bar.

En el primer momento no se dio bien cuenta. Su primer movimiento fue de satisfacción; entonces era cierto que la noche antes un chico no lo había dejado descansar. Todo explicado, era más fácil volver a dormirse. Pero después pensó en lo otro y se sentó[10] lentamente en la cama, sin encender la luz, escuchando. No se engañaba, el llanto venía de la pieza de al lado. El sonido se oía a través de la puerta condenada, se localizaba en ese sector de la habitación al que correspondían los pies de la cama. Pero no podía ser que en la pieza de al lado hubiera un niño; el gerente había dicho claramente que la señora vivía sola, que pasaba casi todo el día en su empleo. Por un segundo se le ocurrió a Petrone que tal vez esa noche estuviera cuidando al niño de alguna parienta o amiga. Pensó en la noche anterior. Ahora estaba seguro de que *ya* había oído el llanto, porque no era un llanto fácil de confundir, más bien una serie irregular de gemidos muy débiles, de hipos quejosos seguidos de un lloriqueo momentáneo, todo ello inconsistente, mínimo, como si el niño estuviera muy enfermo. Debía ser una criatura de pocos meses aunque no llorara con la estridencia y los repentinos cloqueos y ahogos de un recién nacido. Petrone imaginó a un niño – un varón, no sabía por qué – débil y enfermo, de cara consumida y movimientos apagados. *Eso* se quejaba en la noche, llorando pudoroso, sin llamar demasiado la atención. De no estar allí la puerta condenada, el llanto no hubiera vencido las fuertes espaldas de la pared, nadie hubiera sabido que en la pieza de al lado estaba llorando un niño.

*

Por la mañana Petrone lo pensó un rato mientras tomaba el desayuno y fumaba un cigarrillo. Dormir mal no le convenía para su trabajo del día. Dos veces se había despertado en plena noche, y las dos veces a causa del llanto. La segunda vez fue peor, porque a más del llanto se oía la voz de la mujer que trataba de calmar al niño. La voz era muy baja pero tenía un tono ansioso que le daba una

Dismissed, I can't help but watch them. The woman is about my height, but full-bodied, full-hipped beneath her soft skirt, put together in a manner that does not, for once, bring to mind the word *beefy*. She gives off a fecundity we dancers don't give off. A whitened mound of flesh swells above the rim of tight fabric at the back of her dress, a mound Ridley's fingers appear upon sporadically as he organizes their movements. Her neck is bare; her hair is short and dark, and she has almost a round face, with full, expressive lips. The beret slips back from her forehead as Ridley pivots her. They laugh. I light a cigarette, and then I see somehow she's got one lit, too; it appears in the hand that rests upon Ridley's shoulder. As they turn, the cigarette exhales a tail like a sigh that threatens to wrap around them but instead vanishes. She does not look in the mirror at herself, she looks solely at Ridley, and soon he is looking only at her.

And it strikes me that, after all, this is what a dance between a man and a woman is all about.

It's 2:00 A.M. by the time we get out of there, into a street and a skyline nothing like New York. No traffic, no cabs, no cars—just the odd clunker, circa 1960, parked before buildings that are unlit, stunted, clumped low in jagged rows. Ridley takes off—we can see the theater complex from here, rising like a pink city on Bunker Hill, and we start to walk toward it. We look suddenly ridiculous in our after-hours dancerly getup—his boots and my Lycra and leather, his hat, my long scarf. At the corner, Ridley turns back once to look at the bar, and I know what he's thinking: That had to be a mirage. Because it's so empty and weird, it takes Ridley a while to notice I'm giving him the silent treatment. There are signs in Spanish and Korean strung along Broadway, the wide, vacant avenue we are traveling, where Ridley is preoccupied with locating a cab.

"You have to call for them here," I say, finally. "They don't cruise."

"Oh, Joanna, you're wrong," he says. So we keep walking.

"We're going to be killed."

He ignores me.

"Gunned down in the street. By a gang."

"Shut up," he says. "Why didn't you say something back at the bar?"

"I wanted to get out of there. If we'd stayed there one more minute, I'd have been going home alone."

Ridley laughs. "She's too old for me."

"That's right, you like them young. That's what you liked about me, isn't it?"

"Are you kidding? You almost got me arrested, moving into my place. You were a baby."

"Just what you wanted. Somebody too young to make any demands on you. No distraction from your hundred hours a week at the theater."

Ridley stares at me. "I don't want to spend a hundred hours a week at the theater anymore."

"Well, I do," I say.

This is a difficult discussion for us: words are not the tools we work with. Even within the studio we're told what to do with grunts, beats of 1 2 3, sign language—and we learn to talk to each other the same way.

Ridley shifts his weight, looks away from me. "When I visited Don last month in Pittsburgh, he was back living with his parents, sleeping in his old bunk bed, black light posters on the wall." He stops talking for a minute, and I think that's it, but then he looks back at me and goes on. "Don was a great dancer. But I want some other things now, too, Joanna. And so will you, baby, so will you."

I stand there.

Ridley stands there. "How much do you love me, Joanna?"

But in that minute all I can think of is my new contract and my *Bugaku* kimono hanging in the dressing room and the batch of Japanese movies Ridley rented so I could study how the actresses held their heads and how they used their eyes. He'd coached me in the studio, too, until my legs and arms were boneless and rubbery, but my hands stiffened like blades, angular and dangerous, silent protest beneath all that submission. I stand there too long, and then Ridley gives me his back, starts up again, the heels of his boots going *thwack, thwack, thwack,* the echo ricocheting around us, and I have the same panicked sensation I had when I first took company class, which was something like, Shit, I'm going to die.

I am led by the courtiers in their elaborate kimonos onto the stage where Nilas stands, already there in his white tights, torso done up in the theatrically orange Pan-Cake that will wend its way over me by the end of the ballet. For this evening and this purpose my hair has been looped and coiled and stuck through with sparkling metal flowers and my eyes have been painted with the slashing upward lines that make me a beautiful Japanese woman. For *Bugaku* is the dance of a young Japanese couple on their wedding night, the carnal bedroom dance. I stand there, center stage, facing front, swathed in some gauzy sheet of material, and at the moment of everyone's arrested attention, Nilas whisks the cloak off my body. I am not naked, but the illusion is that I am, costumed in an opaque body stocking and a white petaled bikini.

Then Nilas and I begin to dance the slow, languorous series of connections and extensions that suggest our wedding night consummation. Like balsa bent into a bow, I am rocked into an impossible backward *C,* Nilas holding my arms and one leg above us, stringing me up. Then I am lashed beneath his body. My leg is extended high and pressed between us like a sword. Our pelvises meet and pulse. The audience takes a collective breath. I let my head roll back. Then my arms. My tiny headdress grazes the floor, and from this inverted, disorienting posture, I see Ridley staring at me from the wings. His expression is hard to fathom, and for a moment, as Nilas rotates me almost parallel to the floor and almost at its level, I try to fathom it. But then Nilas is pulling me upright, pulling me further into the dance, and I don't look for Ridley again.

Don Quixote

He sat, with Igor Stravinsky, on a little bench by the mirrors at the front of the studio, cameras and cables, barrels of lights around them. They were filming a rehearsal of *Movements for Piano and Orchestra.* Balanchine watched as the dancers took their places, Jacques holding the hand of the girl who was to replace his usual ballerina, whom he felt had betrayed him by becoming pregnant just before the ballet's premiere. This girl was almost as tall as Diana, but very young, seventeen, with a long neck and a delicate, almost doelike face that strained as she sliced into her arabesques penchées. She had a fearless way of moving, throwing herself into the steps as if she didn't care about falling, as if she wanted to fall, and he could not stop watching her. He had seen her in the hallways of his school and now she was here in the studio, doing the adagio he had made for Diana and Jacques, an adagio that looked just that much different now, and the difference was exhilarating to him. It always started like this: a girl held her head a certain way or unfolded her leg so, and he would find it interesting and want to use, want to own. They still had a few days before the ballet's premiere. He would rework some things. He felt Stravinsky shift on the seat beside him. "George, who is this girl?" Without taking his eyes from her, Balanchine answered him. "Igor Fyodorovich, this is Suzanne Farrell. Just been born."

He wanted to see her in everything at once. She took on role after role of Diana's—*Agon, Apollo, Liebeslieder Walzer*—fifteen new ballets in a season. She could do anything. She was his pussycat-fish. Fast like a cheetah, brilliant like a dolphin. Her skin was so white it seemed to absorb all the light of the stage, and he wanted the lights always to be on her. Let her drain them. Her small head reminded him of Tanny's, the long, tapered legs like Tanny's, too, blades of scissors. She had already a stage presence fully realized, more fully realized than her technique, which was still immature, and for which she was always apologizing. He brushed her apologies away. He had seen every dancer in the world, and he understood what he had before him.

He and Tanny had a large apartment, for which he had assembled props as if it were a stage—a giant brass pendulum, an elaborate French chandelier, an early American weather vane, two pianos, blue silk couches that had been part of an old Western movie set. Because the polio had divided her from everything that had once enchanted her, he had made it his mission to provide her with enchantment. They had no TV in the living room, only a phonograph, and he brought in the ironing board to do his shirts while he listened. Tchaikovsky, violin, the piece he would do for Suzi. Tanny's face was rapt, tilted away from him and the heat of the white shirts he stacked by her wheelchair. Her face was still beautiful, but it was haunted for him, rising as it did like a tulip above the long, desiccated body and limbs. Not only was she his wife, his fourth wife, but she had also been his ballerina, before the polio took the power of movement from her. He looked down at the bleached fabric, the blank white shirt. He hated to see any of his dancers after they had aged, their beautiful features crumpled, pinched, or bloated. It was like looking at the debris left by an explosion, and it was unbearable for him. He would rather just remember. But Tanny was here and she was young and the yearning in her face made him weak. He went into the kitchen for a glass of tea, and he stood there to drink it.

In rehearsal Suzanne would follow him—*this? this?*—wanting to please him, giving shape to the shapes he suggested, almost always knowing how to fill out the shorthand, struggling with the steps and then plunging through, figuring out what he wanted and how to make her body give it to him. He would wait, Gordon, the pianist, playing a certain passage from the Tchaikovsky over and over, and then he'd sketch out the series of steps, his sleek hair brushed back from his high, balding forehead, wearing the string tie and the American Indian bracelet his third wife, Maria Tallchief, had given him. He was shorter than Suzanne when she stood on pointe, which meant that he could never partner her onstage, yet in the studio he could partner her better than anyone. Their bodies fit together. Jacques watched. What he made for her and for himself, Jacques would do. She followed, her hair in a ponytail, no makeup, skimming unadorned through the steps. On the day of her school audition three years before, she had danced a little number for him from her ballet recital in Cincinnati; now, she danced his choreography alone. He demonstrated and she followed him, *this? this? Yes.* He would have Jacques put gray in his hair at the temples; she would wear her hair loose. Ballet would be called *Meditation,* and hidden in it was his unspeakable confession. He was fifty-nine. She was eighteen.

The shade in the bedroom was rolled partway up, and the street-light made shadows of his clothes as he dropped them. Tanny was asleep, her face turned toward him on the pillow. She had the profile of an Etruscan queen—noble and serene. He gazed at her dark flesh, her arms, the beautiful waist he had grasped in rehearsal a thousand times as he created on her *Metamorphoses, Western Symphony,* and *La Valse.* It happened again and again, without him willing it—the body, the desire to create for that body, the desire to possess that body, the marriages, four of them, each wife then disappearing from his life like vapor as he found himself drawn to the next. He had been with Tanny the longest, her illness and his obligation to her binding them together. He had made dances for her where her legs had flown, sliced, whipped faster than the ribbons of her costume. Now her legs were stilled, like this.

In Hamburg, on the cavernous stage of the Hamburgische Staatsoper, with all the dancers of the opera, directing *Orpheus and Eurydice,* he watched Eurydice fade, again and again, as they rehearsed the swirling turn with which Orpheus looked back at his love, unable to resist making certain she followed him out of hell. The trapdoor on the gilded ramp would open, the elevator sucking her away, as Orpheus watched helplessly from the ramp's summit. At the opera house he was George Balanchine, the world's greatest living choreographer. In his hotel room later, looking out at the spire of St. Michael's, he was only a man, with his own Eurydice, the one in the body he too had not been able to bring out of hell.

She took his class every morning—not all his dancers did—he knew the complaints, he was too fast, too difficult, he gave too many repetitions, he didn't properly warm them up. He ignored the complaints, did what he wanted. He needed his dancers to move quickly, speed of light, what were they waiting for, what were they saving themselves for, this was the now, it was all they had, the fleeting present. And so he would make them do and do. He had his regulars, the ones whose bodies were too young to be broken by anything yet. He stood by Suzanne at the barre, always, to observe her execution, which then became for him the exemplar. The studio grew humid as the class progressed, but Suzanne never perspired, never panted, she was his alabaster goddess. He could barely look away from her, but when he did, he saw in the faces of his other dancers the strain, not so much from the exercises but from his palpable disinterest.

He was dreaming. Tanny was in the iron lung again, it was dark, warm, the hiss the hiss of the steam irons in the laundry on Seventy-fifth Street. He woke in the living room of the Apthorp, on the sofa where he had taken to sleeping, and lit the cigarettes he had stopped smoking eight years ago in Copenhagen. There he sat by Tanny in her iron lung during the day, his ballet company gone on to Stockholm without him and then back to New York. He'd wanted to get them home, to get out of Europe. He had worked on the Continent for Diaghilev after leaving Russia in 1925, and he knew the streets and buildings of this world. It was a dark world, old and full of plague, and he should not have taken Tanny there. He was terrified and bewildered and guilt-ridden, superstitious enough to believe God had smitten them because he had loved Tanny while he was still married to Maria, and He had chosen polio to smite them as cosmic irony: George had danced with the fifteen-year-old Tanny for a March of Dimes benefit; he had played Polio itself, menacing her with his dark cape as she sat in a child-size wheelchair. At night he'd sit with her doctor in the restaurant by the Blegdems Hospital and drink shot after shot of vodka, cigarettes between each shot, as if a big enough cloud of drink and smoke could blow off the curse he felt sure he had brought to her. Her doctor had become his priest, absolving him with diagrams of the polio virus, whose sponged shape had prompted the fevers so acute they were hallucinatory. He put out his cigarette. In Copenhagen, he too had been feverish, and the red flower on the sill of their hotel room had opened its petals like a beak and spoken to him: You will be punished.

Now he left Tanny at home to come twice a week to the apartment Suzi shared with her mother and sister, this apartment like a girl's jewel box, crammed with beads and trinkets above which the ballerina spun, sublime. The trundle bed in the living room already crowded with furniture, the two beds in the bedroom, the general close quarters, were all testament to the sacrifices made for Suzi's ambition. He came here because he could not stop himself, even though here Suzi was only a girl with an elastic headband hunched over her Monopoly properties, the daughter of a meatpacker, a teenager who had not finished high school because of the demands he made on her; he had given her so much repertory to dance it had consumed her. What was left of her was an eighteen-year-old in a cotton shift who could not get through the Cervantes book he would use as the libretto for his new ballet, but it didn't matter, she didn't need to read, she didn't need to think, he would tell her what to do, what to think, what to feel, what to dance. What he dreamed for her, they would feed on together. They sat at the dining room table with her mother and her sister and played mah-jongg or canasta or rummy.

He showed Tanny the gold-buckled shoes that had been made up for him in the costume shop, the shoes he had now begun wearing in rehearsals to give him the tottery balance of the old man Don Quixote. Tanny seldom came to the theater anymore, but he talked to her always about the ballets. This one would be full-length, and in it he fought imaginary windmills with his sword, rode a wooden donkey exploding with firecrackers, rose on an elevated bed toward heaven in his death scene, transformed his servant girl into his lady Dulcinea. He had brought home none of Suzanne's props, only his own. He never spoke to Tanny of his feelings for Suzi—and he and Suzi never discussed his wife. He felt he had two lives, one with each of them, but they each had only one, with him. When Tanny came to Lincoln Center to see him dance *Don Quixote,* what would she see? He had not been on the stage for ten years, and this was his moment to occupy that space and plane with Suzi, the difference in their ages and their heights all accounted for in this tale of a simple man with his oversized vision, this man who transformed the mundane into the magical. He had done the ballet for Suzanne, but the story of Don Quixote was really his own—that of Georgi Balanchivadze, who came to America in 1933 and imagined classical ballet out of nothing—out of whatever arms and legs he found there.

❧

Under the hot stage lights he knew he looked magnificent—the buckled shoes, the plates of armor, the cotton beard, brows, and mustache—the old man, the befuddled dreamer, and he was there with Suzi, her hair full of flowers and ribbons, the little bones of her chest bared by the low neckline of her costume. She bourréed toward him, and he extended his arm to her. It was the first night and he was full of mistakes—his sword tangled itself in her skirt and he struggled to retrieve it; he forgot to raise his arms in port de bras and Suzi had to lift them for him; at one point he forgot entirely what was next and she had to reach over his shoulder and guide him in the right direction. She was his Dulcinea, his vision and his benediction.

❧

He stood in the wings as she danced the third movement of *Symphony in C*. He had not made the role for her, it was made seventeen years ago for another dancer, but he did not care about other dancers now, past or present. He had used their bodies through the years without knowing that he was marking time, making dances as he waited for her arrival, waited for her, the one who would most fully embody them. Suzi had no understudy. If she could not dance, he did not want to see the ballet. She was the moon crossing the heavens.

❧

His older ballerinas started leaving the company, first one, then the next, then another. Let them leave. He gave them his ballets. If that wasn't enough, then go. He had a right to love.

24

~e

One night he dreamed Suzanne appeared to him naked and sat on his bed, her body glowing orange as if radiated by a piece of coal. Without rousing Tanny, he rose and knelt before her shape. In the lantern of it, his hair shone black as if he were a young man again. He found his skin had smoothed, his features had regained the faintly Asian cast he'd lost somewhat as he'd aged. He opened his shirt to bare his young chest to her. The soles of her feet brushed at his knees, and he saw the shadow between her thighs; it was an invitation, but he could not any further undress.

~e

Suzi and Arthur Mitchell stood, waiting, Arthur's hands on his hips, Suzi working on her pointe shoe, picking at the elastic strap sewn to the heel of it. He looked at his own laced shoe. Something was not right. *Do again.* He followed the profile of Suzi as she moved, the snag in her tights that ran like a shaky ladder up the inside of her thigh and slid beneath the bottom of her leotard. She would wear her hair down for this ballet, her costume a fringed bikini over a bodysuit, something like her costume for *Bugaku,* but more striptease. He had watched her last night in that ballet, watched the leg unfold before her, knee almost to nose, before she let it rest upon the shoulder of Eddie Villella. Eddie bent her backward, the leg still high, until the points of her headdress grazed the back of her costume. She had yielded to him utterly, her body opened like a blossom. Suddenly, he knew what he was looking for. Arthur's hands would not touch Suzi, she would do pas de deux on her own, his body close but not enclosing her, his hands approaching her body but never arriving.

Arthur would wear little costume, would be almost naked, his black flesh against hers as great a taboo as Balanchine's great age.

He waited for his injection in the white bed of the Zurich spa where he had come to take the cures meant to stave off dying, or what presaged dying—the face of age. The bones stood out in his face, the nose had grown wise, the hair had lost its color. It was an enormously dignified face, but no longer young, and he no longer liked to look at himself or to have Suzi look at him. His body, too, had changed, filling up with weight, which he did not like but could not remedy. He winced as the nurse gave him the injection, the extracts from sheep testicles that promised to return to him his youth but instead delivered to him the scrapie virus that would, over the years, make spiderwebs of his brain. He dreamed, now, not of his death, but of his first marriage, to Tamara, in the chapel of the Theater School. He was eighteen, she was sixteen. She had been his first muse, and he knew no more about her than what he could see, which was all he felt he needed to know. On her, after school, he had created the experimental dances for his Young Ballet. He had worn his black hair slicked back, put kohl on his eyelids, no longer the rat, the little boy with a facial tic and an overbite. They had had an apartment on the Moika Canal. In the bedroom, only a bed and a chair. She had hair the color of a yellow leaf, which she had bobbed and given a marcel wave, and she would slowly disrobe for him. It was dark, October 1923.

"I can't accept this," she said.

He took from her the pearl ring surrounded by diamonds and

hurled it across her small dressing room, where it pelted the row of her costumes and seemed to catch on the thick tulle of the skirts before falling. He felt his face contort with anger and misery. He knew he was not only an old man but an old man with a chorus of divorced wives and one not-yet-divorced wife, and this ring was therefore a fraud, paste and glitter, a promise with no teeth. To his terrible face, she said, "All right, I'll wear it," and she crouched down on all fours in her beautiful makeup and elaborate tutu to grope beneath the costume rack, the brocade and the velvet and the sequins and the tulle roiling above her like an angry sea. As she bent, he saw what he should not, the long seam knitting the back of her tights, the cotton crotch at the costume's bottom, the scarred and pitted soles of her pointe shoes. He snapped shut the empty jewelry box he held in his hands.

He sat on the gilded Wild West couch and Tanny sat by him in her wheelchair in the living room of this apartment, so different from their first one together on Seventy-fifth Street, with the two black pianos, the furniture from the Museum of Modern Art, the Baccarat vases, the toaster oven where he had melted Mallomars on foil to make a special dessert. He had loved to buy her things, had loved to adorn her, with shoes, handbags, cologne, the elaborate wired and feathered headdress for *Bourrée Fantasque;* he had loved her wit, her feet, the European slope to her nose. But he had stopped looking at her, and she had not stopped looking at him. At home he felt her watch him, his profile, the way he stood, the line of his leg when he sat and crossed one over the other, the cuff of his trousers raised slightly above the ankle. Even now she watched him. He spoke. After fourteen years, he was leaving Tanny and her wheelchair, the jack-in-the-box that shut into it everything that had been her life. It opened its lid a crack and spoke to him: You will be punished.

~≈

It was March, his first night alone in his new studio apartment, which was bare, functional, a reprimand. He took out his ironing board and began on a shirt to comfort himself. One shirt, two, three. Beneath the blue cambric of his cowboy shirt he saw a shadow ripple. He ran the iron in a wide swath and the shadow disappeared. He put the shirt on. Tanny had been sick for a year when he had first left her side to work again, on a revival of *The Seven Deadly Sins.* In the last scene, he had his ballerina vault in her despair through a closed window, the foil tearing into jagged shards as she broke through it. He buttoned his shirt. Pride. Envy. Avarice. Gluttony. Sloth. Anger. Lust.

~≈

Now he was almost always with Suzanne. She met him each morning for Danish and coffee, and together they walked to the theater for the daily rituals—class, rehearsal, costume fittings. He knew her hands and feet and the contours of her torso and the shape of her head, but he did not know her body the way a man knows a woman. He had never seen her naked, had never put his hands beneath her clothing to the parts of her that pulsed. He would sate his desire for her in rehearsal as he bent, folded, grasped at her body, drew it to his, their limbs tucking together or stretching languidly alongside one another, leg to leg, arm to arm. Before each performance he came by her dressing room to inspect the bouquets massed to the mirrors, his tributes. After curtain, she dressed in one of her gauche teenage prom gowns and he took her to Le Cirque, the Plaza, the Russian Tea Room. When he was unable to escort her to and fro, he had his assistant Eddie do it; he needed to be certain she was never alone, she was chaperoned always, preserved for him.

He watched as she went into the canteen, filled with other dancers. She looked at and spoke to no one, and no one spoke to her. They were glass; she was diamond.

He paced from the music on the stand to the music laid sheet by sheet on the wood floor, and he was not hearing the refrigerator, the clock, the street traffic, or seeing the room with its single bed, the blinds green like the visor of an accountant. Instead, he heard Fauré, Stravinsky, Tchaikovsky, and the white paper with its long black lines quivered. To this music, he would make a ballet about jewels—emeralds, rubies, diamonds—the acts in ascending order, correspondent to the rarity of the gems. The cuffs of his shirt flapped as his hands sketched the grand movement that would close Act III, the girls in concentric circles, the principals revolving in the center, precious stones in a setting held up to the light. The ballerina's costume would be gold brocade, white cloth, and tulle, the fabric heavily encrusted with faceted pieces of diamondlike glass. *Yes.* He would borrow the jewels from his friend Claude Arpels, spread them before Suzanne as he made her this gift, better than jewels. "What do you want to be?" he would ask her, and she would say, as she always did, "I want to be whatever you want me to be."

On the stage her presence was so large and her diamond tutu so gilded and stuck with glass he felt himself diminished, a stone instead of a body pressed into his spot in the wings. When the czar came backstage at the Maryinsky Theatre to greet the children from the evening's ballet, he had felt this way. The boys were lined up in the wings, still in costume, fidgety and trembling. It was in his coaches emblazoned with the royal insignia that the boys had traveled from the school to the theater. It was his purse that paid for the silver-buttoned overcoats that kept them warm in winter. Nicholas paused by Georgi and gave him a chocolate wrapped in foil, a treat that outlasted the czar. Suzanne pivoted in Jacques's arms, then dove into her trademark arabesque. George shivered in the first wing. The czar had been stolen from them, stolen from Russia, and how they had suffered.

"Oh, dear," he said to her. "You don't want to do that." He felt ill with fear.

She was standing before him, holding a paper, an offer letter to dance on TV, the kind of thing Nureyev did, just that kind of thing. Her hair was down, damp and long and thin and flat across her cheek, along her shoulder. She had come to him after rehearsal, he could smell the perfume he had given her to wear, the scent he grazed for everywhere, down every hall, in every elevator. He took the letter from her and found his hands shook. "Why do that? You have everything here. I give you everything, best stage in the world, best costumes, best ballets. You don't need to go anywhere else."

This year at the annual feast he hosted for Russian Orthodox
Easter, Suzanne, not Tanny, sat beside him. She was quiet.
Around them were all his Russian friends, émigrés like himself,
all of them now years in America and beached on the front of old
age. They spoke to each other in Russian, with their eyeglasses
and their dentures and their gray hair and their years of experi-
ences that Suzi with her smooth flesh and brown hair did not
have. She did not know Russian, she had not prayed at St.
Vladimir's in Petrograd, she had not walked Nevsky Prospect
nor feared the Bolsheviks. She had not met Diaghilev or Massine
or Gershwin. She knew only him and the New York City Ballet.
She was quiet because she hated to be simply decorative, like the
lilies or the candles stuck into the thick candelabra or the Easter
cakes, the kulitch tall as top hats, iced and jeweled with candied
fruits and flowers. He moved his hand across the tablecloth to
touch hers. In her body lay his resurrection.

In an interview with the press, he announced that he and Suzi
would marry. She would be fifth Mrs. Balanchine, though he had
not divorced fourth Mrs. Balanchine. This they did not discuss, as
they did not discuss the magazine interview, though he knew that
she had read it. What had remained unspoken between them
from the first, because of Tanny, remained frustratingly unspoken between them still.

She looked down at the cheap spoons, out the plate-glass window
of the Empire Hotel coffee shop, at anything but him as he
talked. Recently it seemed to him her face had begun to show ex-

haustion from the strain of remaining interesting to him, the strain of keeping up with him offstage and of being what he needed her to be onstage for *Meditation, Quixote, Jewels,* and for all the ballets that would follow. He was thinking next of *Sleeping Beauty,* the young girl in the castle defended by briars, impenetrable to all. He recounted the libretto to her now, what he remembered of it from sixty years ago at the Maryinsky—the fountains and lake, the fairy boat crossing the canvas made to roil by a special contingent of the czar's army, the thicket of branches magically enveloping the castle. Suzanne picked at her toast, broke off pieces with a fork. She interrupted him. She did not want to see him anymore outside of the theater.

He stopped eating and within a month lost ten pounds. In rehearsal she seemed acquiescent, attentive, anxious to show him that here, at least, nothing had changed, although for him everything was changed; at the end of the day he went home to his room, drank a shot of vodka, and sat in a profound and unusual despair. When his first wife had left him, he had had the second already by his side; when Maria left him, he was falling in love with Tanny; with Tanny, there was Suzanne. It was only when he lost his third wife, Brigitta, to Broadway and to Hollywood, that he had found himself deluged by the loneliness of his boyhood, which he had early on learned to use marriage to dam. He sat in the chair, drank his vodka, shut his eyes. He was ten years old and standing in the wings of the czar's theater in his little garland costume for Act I of *Sleeping Beauty.* On the front of it were cloth petals that had fallen from the garlands themselves, the lengths of plain rope glued with scraps cut into leaves and blossoms. He

32

brushed at the debris, and the floral bits fell slowly into the empty room.

⤚≫

He had once dreamed of being a musician; she had once dreamed of being Diana, chaste goddess of the moon.

⤚≫

She had moved out of the apartment with her mother; yet some nights he went there still, and her mother would comfort him. He had no family, no children with any of his wives, so he had instead adopted the family of each wife. With Suzi's mother he sat at the kitchen table, traced with his finger the waxed flowers of the tablecloth, looked through photo albums, at pictures of himself cooking steaks in this very kitchen, at pictures of each of them holding the cats, proof that he had finally won over Suzi's, who used to twist like a chamois Slinky and vault into nowhere to flee him. Her mother wanted Suzi to marry him, still held out hope it would happen, and it was because of this that Suzi had moved out and that he visited here. She had asked Suzi, "What's so bad about being Mrs. Balanchine?" Suzi was headstrong, she would knuckle under. He left her mother fortified. Suzi would knuckle under.

⤚≫

He spied her going down the hall toward a studio, the long frame of her, the hair in the ponytail, and beside her, smaller like a shadow, a boy from the corps, Paul. He was as delicately boned as a girl, with dark hair, a long nose, and the odd good looks that recalled to George himself as a youth. The boy was an echo, a taunt.

33

They went into the studio, and George followed, looked through a crack in the door to see Paul handling her body. They were rehearsing the adagio from *A Midsummer Night's Dream* for Oberon and Titania; they paused now and then to sort out the trouble, until bit by bit they shook out the yardage of the dance. It was his own dance, and so he could not be jealous of that, as he had stooped, jealously, outside the studio door when Diana had rehearsed, years ago now, with another choreographer. He had gone in then to break it up, but now he watched without interrupting as these two stepped through the fairyland he had not meant to give them.

～⧽

Paul was nothing, a phase, a mere boy. Yet, Paul was with her everywhere—on the bus, at church, at the theater.

～⧽

He dreamt an iron lung rotated slowly on the stage at the theater. Below it someone walked quietly through the rows of empty seats.

～⧽

On the faces of his dancers he saw despair; he had stopped choreographing, he had stopped looking at their bodies, and in the hallways and studios and rehearsal rooms he saw their anxiety and their concern. He thought he would die.

～⧽

She stood by the door in the tulle and feathers of her Swan Queen costume because he would not enter to deliver his compliment, the threshold an electric blue line between them over which he sent his message, *You were wonderful tonight*. For weeks he had not been to see her in her dressing room, but from the wings he watched her still. He could not stop casting her. Despite himself he had to see her dance. Behind her, he saw the hundreds of little florists' cards that bore his name wedged into the frame of her mirror, all that was left of the bouquets he had sent her season after season for the past five years. *You were wonderful tonight* and *tonight* and *tonight* and *tonight*. It would have to end: it could not go on.

In the hotel room in Guadalajara the air conditioner did not quite work. He sat before it in an undershirt, fanning himself to the strain and drone. He was alone here for seven days to get a Mexican divorce from Tanny. Suzi's mother had called him to say Suzi was marrying Paul, she was going to do it, George, you have to stop it. And so he had come here quietly, before going to Europe, to stop it. The city was a dense and noisy and polluted backdrop to his mission, but his determination turned him inward and he did not hear or smell it. Spanish was one language he did not know well, and hearing it only increased his need to speak to a voice he did know. And so he called Tanny to weep into the phone, "I'm sorry, I'm so sorry." The day Tanny had gotten sick with polio in Copenhagen, she had danced both the matinee and evening, and her body had ached so much she had lain on her dressing room floor between performances. By the following day she could no longer walk. Her body had been stolen from her so abruptly it took him years to understand that she would not get it back, that he must go on. When he finally left her, he had felt nothing, but now his guilt stretched out like a lover beside him on the bed and lingered there.

He was in Europe when he heard the news: Suzanne had married.

God did not want him to have Suzanne.

He made a transatlantic call to the office. He would not come back to New York. He would stay on the dark continent and make a small troupe, rule it as Diaghilev had ruled his dancers—like a czar. His assistant Barbara flew to Hamburg, where she sat in his hotel to cajole and plead with him. He raged at her and wept. She had attended the wedding, she had betrayed him, Suzi had betrayed him, he would give it all up, he did not care about New York City Ballet anymore. He ignored the breakfast tray she ordered him, the metal platters. After ten days, she gave up and went home. It would be more than a month before he came back.

He began to sleep at Lincoln Center. There he had his school and his studios and his theater, and he drew comfort from their solidity and their stability. Within these walls he had the power both to create and to crush. If he wanted black costumes, he would have black, if he wanted this girl to do, she would do, if he wanted this tempo, it was played. He stood at his office window and looked out across the plaza to the New York State Theater, the theater he had had built to his specifications, his theater. He would begin to take roles away from Paul, the husband. He would not have him dance on his stage. And as for her, he would have her teach her roles to the other girls. She would not be only one anymore.

~≈

He would defy God.

~≈

He peered through the door of the main rehearsal studio, while she taught the younger dancer her part in "Diamonds." The girl followed Suzanne's movements, avoided looking directly into Suzanne's face. He watched them dance, the one behind the other, and felt what Suzi must also feel, the betrayal of that other body, a shadow inside the movements he had tailored so precisely for Suzi's talents and predilections. He could not have made this dance if not for Suzi. It would have been a different dance. The younger girl looked shriveled and uncertain, bleached by the glare of Suzi's magnificence; Suzi paused, head bent, hands on her hips. He stepped back from the door. When he saw her in the halls later, he would turn and walk the other way.

~≈

In rehearsal, in the one role he had left to Paul, the juggler in Act I of *Don Quixote,* he stood above the boy before the whole company, making him repeat the taxing steps over and over, making the boy stoop lower and lower in his foolish costume as he begged for money from the crowd. No matter what the boy did it was wrong, and yet the boy tried harder. He knew his own cruelty, but he could not stop himself, and there was no one, not even Suzanne, in her pose to begin her solo, who could stop him.

~❧

She came to his office to ask if she should leave the company. He stood three-quarters turned from her, but still he felt the force with which he missed her. He knew she missed him: they had been too much in each other's company, had meant too much to each other, but they had to be two, they could not be three. He and Suzi stood closer together here than they had in months, and he wanted to be alone together with her again. "Shall I leave the company?" For a terrible moment, the spiderwebs in his brain grew taut and thickened. "No." He spoke. "No, dear. But perhaps Paul should go." Yes. That was it. Paul should go. She must renounce him.

~❧

But she would not. It would not happen that way.

~❧

He felt the blood beat in his ears as he looked into Eddie's pained face. The mouth had just delivered the message from Suzanne in her dressing room: either Paul dances in the performance of *Symphony in C* tonight or they will both resign from the company. How dare she threaten him? How dare she put Paul before him here? Offstage, maybe, but not here, not in his theater. He had made dances for Markova, Danilova, Toumanova, Tallchief. Who was she? Only what he made her. He turned to the piano, thick with scores, let his hands fall down like thunder onto the keys, no music at all but a miserable crash, a warning, one he did not heed; he rushed ahead, making the decision that would pitch him and his company into turmoil, that would derail the careers of beautiful girls ready for the attention he could not give, that would stall his own genius for season after season. He lifted his hands from the keys. He would renounce her. He turned back to his assistant, who held himself stiffly for the miserable blow, who already knew what Balanchine would say.

~≈

She was barred from Lincoln Center, from the studios and the theater, effective immediately, her costume taken from her hanger in the dressing room. She was to pack and go. She was no longer an employee of New York City Ballet.

~≈

It would be six years before he could tell her, *I was wrong, I was an old man, you should have had your marriage.*

~≈

He walked the city that night after the gala, which included not *Symphony in C* but its emergency replacement, *Stars and Stripes,* his paean to America, the country where he had flourished and was now prepared to suffer. He could see neither the streets he walked nor the buildings he passed. He saw only that he had lost Suzanne, lost her body, which was more important to him than his own. He was the Don without his Dulcinea, no longer capable of magic, of conjuring dragons and giants and Madonnas, the extraordinary from the ordinary. He was tired. He stumbled slowly along the blocks ringing the theater until he found himself in front of the Apthorp, Tanny's window dark above him. Cars, people, shapes flowed by him, but he did not move. He could not take a single step.

Departure

I've been with Joe a long time, back when he was twenty-two, with his first Ford Foundation grant and a warehouse space. We might not have been ballet dancers, but that floor was still hell on our joints. Frankie and I got down on our hands and knees and laid a new floor ourselves. Frankie was a beautiful dancer, but I was the one Joe made his dances on. I was his muse. *My moose,* he used to call me. I was a big guy, with rounded shoulders and heavy thighs that poured down into absurdly slender calves. Now, of course, I'm nothing. But back then, when I walked into a room, the space I didn't use fell away from me like paper trimmings. It was that quality Joe liked, and the dances he created for me made his name. Joe Alton. I was there when Joe did his first great work, *Departure,* with the dervishing spins and the motif of the bound bodies, some tied to pillars, some lashed upside down to one another, some bent with their wrists manacled. It's still in the rep.

It's late and I know I should go to sleep, but I keep pacing the apartment. We had the place done a few years ago, and it's full of

crown moldings and silk drapes. When we started getting royal-
ties from *Departure,* Joe began to think of himself as a major
player. He wanted more than six dancers; he wanted private
money to enlarge the company. We had these tuxedos custom tailored, and we went out. You should have seen us, two gods in
robes, Joe with his long, dark hair in that ponytail, me smooth as
a yacht. We started with my parents, then moved on to their
friends, and Joe got a look at how some people in this city live.

So I took my money. One of our set designers had a friend,
and he brought in the columns and the paintings. I didn't want
Park Avenue, and it's not, but this place is dressed, no mistaking
it. I had one proviso: our old stuff was to be put in the guest bedroom. A few chairs, the pine table, our old bed with its white
cover. I go in there a lot, I'm in there now. I just sit and stink up
the place with my dope and read. I haven't read this much since
Princeton. Joe never comes in this room.

Joe was living in the Bowery when I met him, in some sublet, a
rathole with a view. He'd dropped into company class one morning at Joffrey; he wasn't even in the company, Arpino had just
given him the okay, and so of course we were all eyeing him, who
is this prick, but he was great. He had a slender face, almost femi-
nine, full of strength, and he had a great deal of technique. Yet at
the same time he was not a classical dancer. His movements were
too heavy; the ground was his medium, not our air. Even now,
after all these years, I'll still occasionally feel a physical aversion to
the style, as if some vestigial ballet self remains, horrified: You
mean you want to look this way? But that day I couldn't take my
eyes off him.

It was dusk that day by the time we got to Joe's place, and we circled each other in his one room, ending up, finally, at the window ledge for the city to see. Joe felt so thin it was like clutching at charred bones. We rocked before that plate of glass, unrushed, Joe stronger than he looked, and tireless, his long hair loose, displayed. Cold came at us off the glass, which looked black and did not reflect us at all, but led to the outside, to the lit perimeters of the Brooklyn Bridge, to the yellowed entrance of the Greene Street subway station. Afterward we lay on the mattress and Joe punched in a cassette tape of the Sam Leavitt music he was working with at the time and told me about his dance. Two seasons later I resigned from the Joffrey and became one of Joe's pillars—the other was Frankie, a defector from Paul Taylor. Who would have thought some redneck from Tennessee could come to New York and snare the two of us?

When Balanchine got sick in 1978, I went off to Princeton. I'd been studying at the School of American Ballet since sixth grade, and for me, with Balanchine's death, it seemed the whole art form had caved in on itself. I thought Mr. B was the last creative genius and ballet would now preoccupy itself solely with preservation. Fuck that, so I studied art history, oblivious to the irony. I piled my room high with books, wore reading glasses, hung out with Terence O'Hearn, who lived in the studio and at any hour of the day or night could be seen plastering some enormous canvas with the pinched, busy figures that constituted his vision of the world. Complex cartoons layered with inside jokes, the canvases sell for six figures today. He's the one I followed back to New York. We'd stand around in the loft all day in our bathrobes, smoking dope, music blaring—I was painted at least a hundred times—one of the big portraits leans in the entry hall here. One night we went to see the Joffrey Ballet doing some not-too-great stuff to the Prince music that shrieked through the loft at home, and I was just young enough and stupid enough to think this was the new frontier. Within a few months I was limbered up and signed on as a principal dancer. I'd gone from immobility to plasticity in short order.

I had Joe help drag the big portrait of me into the guest room last night so I could sit in my chair and look at it. You can't stare at the blue canvas without feeling as if you're swimming into it. It's a Hockney swimming-pool blue, blue stage-set paint partially rubbed with cheesecloth. It's the Sea of Eternity I'm looking at. I've got a beard on, which Terry scrawled in with stubby black Magic Marker. I've got all kinds of shit in my chamber—old sketches, journals, books, some freaky busts done by Terry's art school crowd, photos of my family, a headdress Lucia wore in some Graham ballet.

I'll tell you what I like to read, my old college art history texts— my Michelangelo, my van Eycks, Masaccio, Dürer—the paintings that smash together the worlds of heaven, hell, and earth in an excitable collision. I don't read, I suppose, I just look at the pictures—at marvelous winged Melencolia; at annunciations; at emperors and popes, bankers and burghers kneeling before the crowned Madonnas in paintings they'd commissioned; at Adams and Eves, innocents of all sorts, fleeing the animalistic Judas; at various Christs speared in gilded landscapes surrounded by screaming angels, bejeweled; a charcoal Death straddling a skeletal, plague-ridden horse. Life was a nightmare, a chaotic agony that culminated in death but was followed by the trembling serenity of the godhead.

It's almost too much to look at tonight, and I study instead the jeweled crucifix Frankie's wife, Lucia, gave me when I was first diagnosed. It's a machine-made piece, this century, not particularly valuable, but it's still an article of faith.

~≈

Frankie's at the pinnacle of his career now, with Joe. He can do anything. He's a parody of health and strength, King Triton at age thirty-eight. He comes over every week, and we sit in my white room. *Your chamber,* Joe calls it. We make an underwater journey to the wreck, Frankie and I, talking about our first few years together when we danced in church basements and the two of us pulled in the audience for Joe. Frankie and I have always talked, even if Joe and I couldn't. Frankie came to sit by me at St. Luke's and we talked there, too. We can revisit the past, but we can't divine the future. It's hard to know how long I have, how long Joe has. For now, Frankie's just trying to make the most of the new work Joe's setting on him.

I always got a big kick out of watching Joe work in the studio, as he figured out how to make all the bodies in there do what the tiny bodies in his head were doing. I wasn't the creator, but I took on the sacred and onerous task of interpretation. It's not particularly romantic, actually it's somewhat self-serving of us both, but I guess that's one of the reasons Joe and I stuck together after Cologne. I was a good vehicle because Joe could see his work given a balletic treatment—there was no way I could fully shake my ballet training—and that's why Joe used to give Frankie short shrift in favor of me. Joe worshiped ballet: he'd started too late to be a classical dancer.

I go down to the studio now, sometimes with my goddamn cane, and see the great stuff Joe's working on for Frankie and our newest boy, Eric Gonzalez, and for the two girls we added last year. Joe's after Lucia, too, wanting to do a solo piece for her. Sam Leavitt's already doing the music. Joe's got commissions and college residencies and regisseurial duties lined up for the next three years. It's all in his appointment book in the bedroom drawer. Sometimes I'll open it and stare at his plans: they just go on and on. I can't see the dances, though. There's no way to put them down in a book. A dance is not an image that can be printed and bound, not like a painting. Although, to be fair, even a painting doesn't reproduce that well. The colors are always off, and the real painting, when you see it, almost flattens you with its immediacy and its scale.

Last month I coached Eric in my old role in *Departure,* the executioner turned masked boatman. The dance was inspired by the Beckmann triptych I showed Joe ten years ago, the side panels of carnage and agony trumped by the blue backdrop and glowing boat of the center panel. Most of the ballet is consumed with the writhing, spinning bodies, but in the apotheosis, hooded and draped, wearing a gold armband, I shepherd a boatload of static crowned figures toward the horizon. I'm the only one moving for five minutes. I'd shared the role with several boys over the years, but this time it was different. I wasn't going to be dancing again, and I found myself in the studio wanting to tell Eric more than just the steps but the way I breathed and thought my way through them all. It surprised me a little to understand how much I'd held back when showing other dancers the ropes, jealous of my triumph, as if I could dwell forever within it only if I guarded the role.

Joe had hired Eric last season—we have twenty dancers now,

large for a modern dance troupe—and at the time Eric had seemed largely decorative to me, with his long hair and resolutely unballetic practice clothes—a dress shirt, khakis, and black Nikes. Another boy, like Eli Strauss, for Joe to fall in love with. But I'd misjudged Eric. He could dance. He listened gravely as I moved alongside him, the two of us half-talking, half-marking our way through the steps. He mimicked the tilt of my head, even the placement of my thumbs as I brought my palms to my eyes. But he didn't look like me. It wasn't until I saw him inside my role that I realized how much he looked like Joe, the Joe of fifteen years back. When we did the big turns, Eric shot around in an impossibly low crouch, dancing full-out, his hair a thick, elevated swatch. It was a beautiful dance, and Joe had been no older than Eric when he composed it.

Our first few years together Joe and I would cruise for boys; it was our particular sport, a compulsion and a vanity. We'd drive through the park in my Corvette, or we'd visit the baths and bars where *Übermen* like Nureyev ruled. We'd watched him once, take on boy after boy in a truck parked by the piers in the meat-packing district. We watched each other, too, in those bars. We were proving something—see how lucky you are to have desirable me. Then we'd go home to bed and hammer on each other, crazed. Joe and I were always prone to scenes, like subversive fourteen-year-olds, always afraid the other would walk, always playing at it.

It was hard for him, coming out, and that made it hard for us. It took a few years before we decided on monogamy. I mean, we'd already been living together that long. Joe had gone to an arts high school in Memphis, but beyond its perimeters he was seen as a candy-assed fairy, a Tennessee Williams oddball, a Miss Nancy. I grew up on Park Avenue, and my mother's brother was gay, a regular Joe in the cosmopolitan mix. He took me to my first ballet, Balanchine's *Serenade*. I got one look at the line of girls in their long tutus and that was it. That I knew I was gay by the sixth grade had nothing to do with my uncle or with dancing. That I wasn't afraid to come out or to love Joe had everything to do with both.

But Joe's affair with Eli Strauss was not about play. After Eli joined the company six years ago, Joe's attention was diverted. Eli was not a boy, and he did not look like a dancer. He had an angular face, with a Cro-Magnon brow, sunken cheeks, and a short fringe of bangs like a monk's. It was an ascetic face, arresting. He didn't look American, and he did not have an American way of moving—more European, tensile, stiff-kneed, abrupt. It was not like anything I'd seen in a New York studio before. Joe started to do some things for him, a solo piece, then a whole construction with a story. I knew from Joe's notebook and the electronic music he was listening to around the apartment that the whole direction of his choreography was changing. He was no longer looking at the moose. He wasn't always home nights. I endured it for a while. I'd beat off on my own or go out and find somebody. In rehearsal we'd argue and Frankie would have to step in. I was called to rehearsal less and less, and when I was there, it was Joe and Eli with their coffees during break. But Joe and I never talked about it. Weeknights I'd retreat to Frankie and Lucia's. Adam was just born. I'd walk with him in his little red room, six paces by eight, his stomach against my shoulder, head over the hill, drool down my back. He'd had colic; it was the only position he could tolerate. We were miserable together. On weekends, Joe and I'd dress up in the tuxes, nothing wrong, go Park Avenue partying with the people I'd grown up with, soliciting cash.

We finally had it out one night after one of those parties, 3:00 A.M., in our bow ties and cummerbunds. *You want to fucking destroy me. You're a fascist, Randall. Don't tell me what I can create and who I can fuck.* We trashed our place, screaming at each other, Joe knocking over chairs, trying to pull down a Venetian blind, but that sucker was mounted tight, and at the end of it, Joe sat there looking at his hands, not quite defeated. So I yanked my money out from under the company and went to Europe, to Cologne, the dark city with the black cathedral and the river of soot. I hunkered down in Cologne. The day Joe tracked me there was a great day for me. I don't think he believed he could do it without me. He could have. But he came to Cologne. It stank that day, I remember. We went home, Eli was fired, I endowed the crippled company, I had the apartment redecorated. I was a pig, I was a tyrant, I didn't even know it. Back then I just thought, What a victory.

When boys all over the city started going to St. Luke's, to Roosevelt, to NYU, Beth Israel, Goldwater, St. Vincent's, falling down with the plague, Joe and I got tested. It was winter, and afterward, we went to St. John's for vespers. Without prayer books, we spoke what we knew, and when we emerged, we found outside the church a black night and a white earth. Snow had made equal planes of the street and the sidewalks, and there was no sound, as if all this street and the city behind it were an extension of St. John's. It felt holy and the sky swollen. We stood there. And then around us the white lean-tos that sheltered garbage cans and stoops shifted and cracked; in the imperceptibly disintegrating landscape, the snow crests and figurines that rose off auto hoods and antennae and the spiky newels of fences and the cornices of roofs slowly sank and vanished. Beneath them, stained deeply, lay pedestrian things, terrifying things.

Frankie and Lucia had the party after the opening tonight in their loft, an ugly, vacant space near the meat district. I'd put up the 20 percent for the place, and every time I get a look at it, I find it hard to believe I'd had to fork over more than a dollar. But tonight it seemed their loft was a church, a huge white space with the masks Lucia'd collected during all her tours hammered into neat rows on one wall. She's a Graham dancer, one of those glamorous creatures with the thick false eyelashes and elaborately wound hair of the goddess herself. Not only do Graham's dancers move like her they look like her. It's like watching Martha's ghosts when you see the company perform. The loft had a few dark chairs, a long, dark table, a black buffet. It was a Puritan church, stripped and unadorned. At the end of it, two bedrooms cowered like shamefaced Catholic chapels, and their interiors were lush: Frankie and Lucia's bed covered in purple velvet, Adam's room a mosaic of toys and red wallpaper. I spent an hour or so in there, too tired to watch Joe gawping at Eric, who wore his hair slicked back from his forehead and a leather vest over his black turtleneck, like some discomfited amalgam of the sixties and the nineties. Joe watched him, that was all: it had been a long time since Joe and I had even fucked, but he knew that I would still care, and that I could still crack my money like a whip. To spare us both, I hunched down at the foot of Adam's bed while he slept, his squadron of model biplanes suspended above us on plastic wires, their underbellies painted ferociously vivid hues. Half the toys in here I'd given him—the Edward Gorey book full of ballet cartoons, a suit of armor I'd bought at an auction, the night-light a strand of Halloween lights with pumpkins and ogres.

When Adam was born, Frankie and Lucia had him baptized at St. John's in the Village. Joe and I were there. I was godfather, and during the ceremony I had one of those moments when I asked, *Why am I a faggot?* I know it's just a given, as much a given of my existence as the fact that I'm big, that my mother's got a wad of money, that I'm dying, but there are times, there are times.

Tonight was the first time in fifteen years we didn't host the party to open the season; next month will be the first Christmas. Even up to last year, I did it all—the swagged lemon leaves and pepper berries, the twelve-foot tree thick with ornaments, the pears rolled in sugar and toothpicked into topiaries. We had sit-down dinners for twenty-four, the table a bowling alley of crystal and silver, so Joe could revel in how far he'd come from the paneled rec room on Waring Road with the Sears artificial tree. Balanchine was famous for his masterpiece Easter, with his buffet of towering, elaborately frosted cakes. His focus was resurrection; my focus was birth—I gave a life to Joe.

All last week I'd watched Joe working with Eric, doing the final coaching, polishing him up. Joe in his uniform, the muscle T-shirt, flapping baggy pants, remaining hair tied into a slick ponytail, demonstrating the steps, *yes, yes!* recasting Eric's arm, moving before him, *Deeper, step right, pull up.* Out front, in the dark audience tonight, his eyes followed Eric stage right, stage

left, attention riveted on his muse, which was as it should be. Forget films, forget photos, forget the painstaking labanotation in the
dance archives, there is no substitute for this—memory and con-
tact. Eric was doing my dance, the one I'd taught him, the one Joe
was teaching him, the one Eric would someday teach. The living
art. Eventually, I watched the stage myself and saw it was full of
Joe's phantoms and mine and Eli's and all the young, beautiful,
supple, agile bodies who had moved through these dances. The
night Balanchine died, his company danced at Lincoln Center
and his spirit was everywhere in the theater. His dancers saw him
on the catwalks, in the wings, felt his breath behind them, pushing them forward, his hands on their backs.

Sam will make the music and Frankie will run the company;
yeah, he'll be a goddamn preservationist, but, after all, Balanchine's company has survived, and Graham's.

I get up and leave my chamber for the bedroom. I'm still
wearing my tux. Getting the thing off is more than I can manage
at this hour. Earlier tonight Joe had to manipulate the anatomy of
it onto me—stuff my limbs where the limbs should go, solder the
seams with the zippers and buttons. During the ordeal, I saw Joe's
face crumple, then grow resolute.

I have a phobia about sleep, so I sit on the chaise and watch Joe
in that elaborate bed all by himself. He's still. A section of some
1500s French tapestry hangs at his head—a stitched panoply of
figures and animals, lords and ladies, stags and hounds, trees and
flowering shrubs, all the beauty of the world.

Wili

$\mathcal{I}$*'m a Wili,* which basically requires me to stand on one foot with the other one pointed behind me for about the whole of Act II, and though I'm watching Sylvie Guillem, who's guesting with us this season and whom I practically worship, I'm also keeping an eye out the rehearsal door for Michael, who's flirting with this girl who just defected from City Ballet. I can see his form moving back and forth in front of the vendors out there in the hall and the girl leaning against the side of the Coke machine, collapsed with laughter at Michael's witticisms. All of which I've heard, ha, ha. He and I are supposed to go out tonight, but now I'm wondering. I've known Michael forever—we were on scholarship together in the company school—but we've never really gotten it together, mostly because I already have a boyfriend. But right now all I want to do to Jack is punch his face in.

Because this is just a run-through, I cheat and put the foot behind me flat on the floor. We've got on our long rehearsal tutus so we can keep the right amount of space between us in our lineup, it's always a surprise how much room these things take up, but anyway that's how I can get away with standing flat-footed: nobody can see. But then I feel guilty. Even though nothing about this rehearsal is full-out, even the score is reduced from senti-mental orchestral lushness to a plinky upright piano rendering, Sylvie is giving it her all. She's Nureyev's protégée, on loan from the Paris Opéra, and she's totally gorgeous, with this long neck and the sway-backed legs that give her a swooping line nobody can match, and when she turns to face her Albrecht and the line of us behind him, her eyebrows are raised with the mock anguish that belongs to a performance Giselle. When Baryshnikov lifts her in the long diagonal series of arabesques sautés, it looks as if he's pulling her down out of the air rather than raising her up into it. I feel my mouth open, and then our line ceremoniously switches feet, which confuses me for a moment since I'm standing on both of them. Our big move and I screw it up.

It's not that I'm not a good dancer, I think I'm okay, but once I had this idea that I'd be great, and I'm having a hard time let-ting go of the idea. A few seasons watching dancers like Sylvie and some of the comers in the company and I've gone from thinking, I can do that, to something like, I don't know if I can do that. An ominous trajectory, especially in this company. Since joining four years ago I've found myself relegated to a rank some-where between corps de ballet and soloist, but this past year I've bottomed out. I haven't been cast in anything but ensemble roles all season, which Jack thinks serves me right.

I tug at my sweater, do a few relevés, watch as two columns of dancers cross, kicking up thin layers of tulle as they pass each other by, staking a new pattern on the floor. We're blocking Al-brecht, keeping him from Giselle, forcing him to dance to his death for breaking her heart, even though she doesn't seem to appreciate this exacting revenge. *Au contraire.* Stupid girl, she doesn't want him to die. But we're girls who've died of broken hearts the nights before our weddings, and so we dance on in our tutus and veils. I feel the features of my face gradually assume the fixed attentive port Jack likes to call "glazed." "You all get that deadened look on your faces," he once said, talking about us ballet dancers. "You look like a bunch of zombies." Jack is a show dancer, little honor, mucho dinero. At least, compared with our pay. But he's terrific at what he does, he's a much better dancer, for example, than Michael, who's actually pretty terrible. But Michael doesn't seem to care. He's all wild feet, flapping arms, and ignorant exuberance. You can tell he thinks he's doing just fine, thank you. But he's a boy and they need boys, ballet companies always need boys, so that's why I'm standing in a line of Wilis and he gets to play Hilarion (which is, I'm compelled to point out, mostly a walking role) and have his picture taken for the gala program.

I told my four-year-old niece, Katie, that Wilis were fairies. Why scare her and tell her how hateful disappointed women can be, even from the grave? She'll find out soon enough. I took a cab uptown to their apartment in the Eldorado last weekend, right after a costume fitting. My sister Alison has this huge place. We horsed around in the kitchen for a while. I described the costume to her, talking about how they had to tack the veils to the backs of the dresses so we won't trip. Katie listened for a long time before she asked what I was supposed to be. I'm planning to go uptown again tonight, after rehearsal. Alison's husband died a few months ago, and she needs the company.

Maybe it's because I'm wearing the wrong stuff today (my baggy sweater hangs over the waistband of my long tulle skirt, hiding my ratty leotard) and that's why I'm having a lousy afternoon. Or maybe it's because my hair didn't come out right the last time—the color's too brassy. Maybe it's the fight Jack and I had last night, or that my pointe shoes are too hard, or that I'm a Wili instead of Myrtha, the lead Wili, forget Giselle. I'm just starting to think about faking a leg cramp and slinking my way to the back wall when Sylvie runs by the line of us, her arms pitched behind her, head thrown back, her face hollowed with the intensity of her concentration. Okay, that's why she's the star.

I live in Chinatown, a sole *low faan,* a white barbarian, in a small box with a view of the bridge. Jack's sitting in my apartment when I get there, his shirt marked with dark spots of sweat. He must have come straight from rehearsal for *Chicago.* He's the dance captain for the show and one of the featured dancers. He's built exactly like a jazz dancer, thick at the shoulders, spare hips, bulky thighs. He gets up from the sofa when I walk in, and he's something to behold—he looks just like a movie star. Women will talk to him anywhere. I saw a woman move in on him at a factory outlet for shoes, where he'd been strutting around in a pair of cowboy boots, knowing he looked pretty hot. Alison thinks he's too good-looking not to sleep around, but all this time I know Jack's only been with me. He's careful that way. His body is his prize. It was *months* before he'd make love to me, even though I fell for him right away. I met him in a jazz class five years ago. We danced some combinations together, and I kept forgetting the steps, distracted by his body, his proximity. But he hauled me along, sometimes by the slick neckline of my leotard. He took me out afterward. I never expected we'd be together this long.

"Still hate me?" he says. He kisses me, kisses me a long time, trying to make me weaken. Another few minutes, and he takes me to the bedroom, but once we're there, he gets distracted by the sight of the big suitcase I've packed. It's sitting up on a bench at the foot of the bed.

"How long are you staying at your sister's?" he asks.

"One night," I tell him, though it sure looks like I've packed for more.

"Don't you have company class tomorrow morning?" He makes a face I can't quite see; I can make out only the change in the angle of his jaw.

"I'll get back for it."

"Sure," Jack says. I can see his face now. It's sour.

Jack always has his mind on his work. He was a small-time jazz teacher who turned himself into the genuine article. You go to see him in *Les Miz* or something and he stands out like an energy-emitting laser. But he got a late start—he was twenty-five by the time he got his first roles, and already he sees it all starting to slip away from him. So he hammers at *me* all the time. He'll check the scale to make sure I haven't gained a pound, put me in a cab uptown to David Howard's studio for extra class. Two years ago, when I was picked for my first soloist role in *Swan Lake,* Jack went nuts. He came to every performance—he was between shows then—telling me next time around I'd be the Swan Queen herself. He's still waiting for that one.

Jack rolls his body on top of mine and makes me put my arms around him. In this moment and this position I start to feel a little guilty about my subterranean plans for tonight. Of course, I'm not exactly going out on a date, but I'm not exactly telling Jack about it either. He's got his mouth on my neck. "It'll have to be a quickie," he says. "Curtain's at seven-thirty." It's Sunday. "One more month of this and I'll be ready for the retirement home. No, I shouldn't say that. I take it back. It's all right. I'm into it." He reaches into the drawer where we keep the rubbers, and then he sits up.

"What's this?" he asks. He's holding a little Baggie with a few pills in it I've managed to scare up.

"Oh, what?" I say. "Like you've never used."

"I'm dancing nine fucking shows a week. I need it to make it through."

"Well, I need it, too."

"What you need," he says, "is to show up for your goddamn classes and rehearsals on time."

"Go to hell," I tell him. All we do now is argue.

Last night we fought because he wanted to know all about who was cast as Myrtha, who was cast as Bathilde, did Baryshnikov look at me at all during rehearsal, did I go up to him and ask him to recommend a coach for me like Jack wanted me to, and then he hit the roof when I said I hadn't. This is exactly what Jack did to make it—he danced the whole time looking left and looking right to see who was doing what better, who was making it, who was coming up behind him. Now that everybody's coming up behind me and passing me by, Jack's gone into action. He's convinced if I hire a coach it will somehow resuscitate my so-called career. He's killing me. He thinks he's the dance captain of my life.

Jack gets up and goes to the bathroom, flushes the pills down the toilet.

Then he stands in the doorway to say, "I don't know what you worked all these years for."

At that, I get out of bed and button my shirt and scream. "Shut up," I tell him. "Shut up, shut up, shut up."

"Katie's asleep," Alison says to me at the door. She's wearing her blue bathrobe, the sash tied loosely around her waist. She's cut her hair, and the ends of it curl into the air at her neck.

"When did you do that?" I ask, trying not to gape at her.

"About two hours ago." She turns, and I follow her inside. "It looks terrible, doesn't it?"

I don't answer.

"I saved the part I cut off," she says. "I figured I could make it into a hair shirt."

"Alison."

She laughs, sort of. The back of her hair hangs down in two points like the bottom of a *w*. "Stop staring at me." She sits down on the couch and opens a piece of newspaper over her head, and I see she's moved her wedding band to her third finger. It makes me tired just to look at her. Papers are spread all over the carpet, and a china teapot and dirty cups sprawl on the little end table. Peter died right here on the floor while Alison watched. He'd suffered a heart attack and died within ten minutes, and afterward Alison turned into a dummy, a grenade with the pin stuck in, eerily inert. Her hair, which has always been pale, is now waxen; even the color of her eyes seems a shade lighter, as if whatever combustion that keeps us alive has been reduced in her. She can't eat. The last time I was over I made her an egg that sat on the plate, even though she told me she knew if she didn't eat she was going to die.

"Maybe I can fix your hair," I say.

"The scissors are in the bedroom," Alison says. "I sat on a sheet and then rolled everything into a ball."

We go down the hall and she sits on the bed while I unwrap the sheet and find the thick-bladed sewing scissors sunk in a pile of blondish hair. Alison loosens her robe and waits with sloping

shoulders, the comforters rumpled around her knees. I edge
around her, snipping; I don't know what I'm doing. Short hairs
float about our faces, and some settle along Alison's arms. Each
time I put my knee to the mattress, the box spring squawks. She
and Peter bought this old iron bed at an estate sale, their wedding
present to themselves. Alison married Peter around the same
time I met Jack, a long time ago. The four of us would go out
drinking together in Chinatown, and then, soused on Tsingtao
beer, careen back to Peter's old apartment (now mine), Peter leaning so heavily on Alison, she'd bend at the waist. We'd take the
mattress off the box spring and crash in a long row, as if we were
in some flophouse; the fumes coming off us could kill any living
thing. But Alison is still alive. As I work, I can see her chest rise
and fall, rise and fall in the blue valley of her bathrobe. And when
she begins to talk to me, I stop flashing the scissors and listen.
She's talking about the day Katie was born, and how she'd
walked in circles in the delivery room, desperate and laboring,
until finally she'd clutched at Peter's shirt collar and dragged his
face down to hers, saying, "Help me," but there was nothing he
could do.

When I'm sure Alison is sleeping, I take the scissors so she can't
do anything weird with them and shut the bedroom door. The
apartment is black. Standing at the tall window, I can see the lit-
up edge of Park Avenue and, past that, the darkness of Central
Park. There is not a sound. This apartment is prewar and solidly
built. I lean against the thick molded window frame and wait in
the vacant room. A timer-set lamp by the sofa goes on, clipping
my reflection up onto the window before me like an X ray. I'm so
sick of looking at myself, my scrawny ridiculous self. It's my little

Baggie of pills that gives me the confidence to go beyond that painful image in the mirror. Sometimes, catching a glimpse in the dressing room mirror at the theater, in full makeup, dark lines slashing outward from my eyes, my narrow tiara set just at the crown of my head, I see the dancer I want to be; and sometimes, staring at myself after a hard rehearsal, seeing my hair long and damp along the edges of my face, my prized gauntness, the strange haggard and dreamy look on my face, I'm also pleased. But it doesn't take a genius to figure out which side of me management was seeing this season. I mean, one minute I'm dancing center stage, and the next it's, Katherine to the backdrop, please.

I've wanted to dance with this company since I was twelve years old, a scholarship student in my pink leotard. By the time I was sixteen, I was the only girl left from my original class. All the others had gotten tired or fat or disinterested. But not me. I was driven and I had been promised a reward for my dedication— and I was rewarded, at first. There was *Swan Lake,* with my feathers and tiara. There would be *Giselle,* with the wings and the white face and the graveyard. But then there was nothing. There was Sylvie Guillem, and I was a girl, an anonymous girl in the back row with her forty sisters. And sometimes not even that. Some days I don't go to the theater at all. I call in to put myself on sick list and then meander around Chinatown, looking at the shop-windowed rows of strung-up, beheaded ducks.

The light by the sofa goes off, and one in the hallway goes on. I get up and go out to this little terrace Alison's got that the rest of Manhattan would kill for. The floodlights are on, and I can just make out the shape of a doll sitting on the glass table at the far end near the potted bushes. I go outside and look at it, shake its hand. Katie has painted its fingernails. Since Peter died, Katie plays incessantly with her dolls and figures, and she stares for long periods at the pictures in her books she cannot yet read. I let go of the doll's hand. Out here, the traffic rushes, heading downtown toward the action. I need to get moving if I'm going to meet Michael. I look back through the glass doors. It's dark in the living room except for the lamps switching on and off. Alison could keep it lit all night, and still death would sit in that room.

The place Michael and I are going to is way downtown, beyond downtown, one of those East Village performance art spaces where they paint the four walls black, hang up a few sets of lights, and that's the stage. It's about as far away as you can get from the Eldorado without crossing water. And Michael makes us take the subway to get there. I don't like to take the subway after dark, but I'm not allowed to say anything about that. Or about modern dance, which I find incredibly boring, but it has this cachet, as if somehow it's more interesting or intellectual than ballet. Michael is always up for the ultracool—even though it's a well-known dictum among us Wilis and swans that a modern dancer is a dancer who just couldn't cut it in ballet.

Anyway, tonight we're seeing Nadia Talbot and Company, and by the time we get there all the seats are taken and we have to sit down front on a row of chairs that's practically part of the stage. I'm wearing this long velvet dress I swiped from Alison's closet and a pair of boots with heels just tall enough to make me feel unsteady, and I feel like I'm on display before this incredibly hip herd rising on the bleachers above us. Michael's hardly looked at me at all, he's been so busy with the tokens and this little flyer with the address, and now he's craning his neck to see who all is here, like there's anybody he knows in the East Village, and I feel like a chump, a velvet-covered chump. Some girl at the end of our row is ceremoniously smoking a cigarette, and when I sit down next to her, she drops the butt on the floor of the stage and begins a monologue. Which makes me think (1) that we've sat by mistake on some of the props, and (2) that this might be the wrong performance. Weren't we seeing a dance thing?

But after she finishes her monologue, which is about all the men her mother went out with while she was growing up, she starts to dance and it's actually not too bad, even when she's joined by this guy who's pretty much limited to a few walks and stoops and to swinging her around periodically, sometimes on the ground, sometimes in the air. This is low-end dance. Undemanding in every way. No technique, all show. And that's when it comes to me: Michael would be good at this.

At intermission we huddle with everybody else at the front door, clouds of smoke hanging toxic in the air and then rising in jigsaw shards above the low roofs around us. Michael sucks authoritatively on the stub of a cigarette he bummed from a guy in a pest-control jumpsuit (some sartorial form of urban cool) and says to me, "Maybe you should think about taking up modern dance, you know?"

"Know what?"

"Since you're not really going anywhere at ABT." He steps on the butt.

"I'm not going anywhere?" I say.

"Well, you've been there almost five years, Katherine. I've already been promoted." He holds up five fingers like I don't know what five means.

I just stand there a moment in what he probably thinks is a contemplative posture, but all I can think about is if Michael thinks this, probably everybody else in the company is thinking it, too. Oh, God, I'm going to have to leave the company before everyone starts to pity me. The door light blinks twice and the audience begins to file back into the theater. Michael starts to go, too, until I hiss at him, "You know something? You've got an ego the size of Las Vegas."

He stops in his tracks. "Why? Because I know I'm good?"

"Good at what? You stink at everything. But you're a boy."

"Why can't you face it? I'm a better dancer than you."

And I don't know what's worse—having Jack think it's all my fault for not working hard enough or having Michael think it's not my fault, that hard work won't help. No. I know what's worse.

"Look, shithead," I say. "I'll be here long after you're tap dancing on *Destination Stardom*."

His face gets red. I'm getting to him—tap dance is really the lowest of the low, right down there with acrobatics.

"I don't even know how to tap," Michael shouts, and I stomp off up the street toward God knows where, and in my moment of anger and terror Michael streaks up behind me and stands me flat against a dark building into a ferociously gymnastic kiss.

I phone Jack at 3:00 A.M. from Alison's hall closet. I sit on a plastic milk crate filled with gloves, press my temple to Peter's fleecy jacket while I listen to the telephone ring at my place. Then I hang up and dial Jack's room at the hotel. No answer. I pull the jacket down off its hanger and hold it to me. It's thick and warm. I try my apartment again. Nothing. I'm not going to talk to Jack tonight. What could I possibly say to him, anyway? I sit there miserably on the milk crate and gaze at all the coats strung up on the horizontal pole. Some big trench coats and suit jackets are hanging toward the back, and I realize Alison has cataloged the closet: Katie's things at the front, Peter's clothing held separate by hangers of Alison's sweaters. I use my foot to push the closet door open. It swings slowly outward, and I see Katie standing there, garbed in her shortie nightgown. We stare at each other.

"There you are," she says.

I'm floored.

"Jack called you." She stands there looking at me, and I get up off the milk crate.

"When did he call, honey?" I take her hand and lead her away from the closet.

"One o'clock," she tells me. "We couldn't find you. Were you in there?"

"No," I say, hoisting her up. Shit. She puts her arms around my neck. That close, I can smell the sweet shampoo Alison uses to wash Katie's hair. At least she's still washing Katie's hair. Katie gives me a little kiss. I grip her tightly, sway with her for a bit before starting for her room. She puts her foot out, and it knocks gently against the hallway walls as I carry her. A pink play tutu swings on the knob of her closet door. I put my finger into the palm of her hand, and she grips it automatically. She has a small, finely chiseled nose, and heavy, silky, Asian hair; we don't look much alike. She sighs and releases my finger, her palm sliding to rest against her baby quilt. I watch her curl into sleep and wonder what Jack's been thinking about since 1:00 A.M. Katie makes a sleeping noise and turns her closed face along her pillow. I put my hand down on the sheet by her neck. Peter and Alison named her after me.

I'm so astonished I actually drink the coffee Alison brings me, though I never drink coffee. She's even brought in a portable aluminum coffeepot, which she plugs into the outlet behind the bureau, as if she expects I might want gallons of the stuff. Then she sits by me on the bed to watch. I have to laugh. "I got laid, Alison," I say, "not drunk." She smiles. "Either one can be a disaster." She leans back, looking bemused, not censorious, and I wonder if we might actually talk. Bad sex is the sort of thing I used to talk about with Alison when Alison was Alison. Bad breakups, too. I want to tell her what's been going on between Jack and me and what I'm afraid is going to happen now. She knows Jack almost as well as I do. I was living with her and Peter when I met him, and when Peter got his big job on Wall Street and they moved uptown, I stayed behind in the Bowery and Jack became my first boyfriend. I want Alison, who's gone to college and come home with her cigarettes and her stories and her birth control devices, to tell me her interpretation of the world. But Katie keeps making sporadic appearances in the guest room doorway, giving us a sort of reversed striptease, flashing her body in its consecutive stages of dress, in a wild hurry to go to morning preschool. So I don't even start.

Instead, I lie down next to Alison and look at the ceiling. I'm tired, and the cracks in the plaster seem to vibrate, to assemble themselves, and to move. Alison told me *she* moves from bed to bed at night, searching for sleep. What does she see, what speaks to her, when she lies in here? I turn my head to look at her and her new short hair standing by her ear. Next to her ear and hair sits a box on the night table, which is filled with books and small objects, and that's when I notice the bookshelves in the guest room have been cleared. Orderly Alison. She doesn't just wander the apartment in her blue bathrobe. She's quietly beginning to

pack up the rooms they don't use much in anticipation of moving. Of course. Peter is dead; the Eldorado apartment will have to be sold. And I'm rich suddenly, with grief, for what she thought her life would be. It's not her fault, it's not what she deserves, but it's what she has to take instead. I'm just about to reach for her hand, when she says, "You'd better get ready for class." After all, she's gotten me up for it. She pushes herself off the bed, and soon I hear her in the bathroom with Katie.

My first month on my own in Peter's old apartment in Chinatown, I was so unnerved, I made Jack, Peter, and Alison stay with me every night. This was when Katie was a baby. We'd put pillows around her on the bed and then sit up in the living room on these godforsaken bits of furniture Peter had in there, doing lines or downing shots of Stoli, the barbarians among us daring each other to eat whatever stuff we'd bought from the vendors on Canal—dried octopus, curried squid, betel nuts. I'd just started to understudy my role as Giselle, and giddy over it, I showed them the dance one night, using Jack as my partner. We did that long line of supported arabesques sautés, and we were so high that Jack twisted us into rubbery, comic contortions, or else, egged on by Peter and Alison's laughter, flipped me up into the air in some spectacularly dangerous configuration, my legs hitting the ceiling. Finally some old lady from upstairs knocked on the door, and I remember how Peter mollified her, speaking to her in Chinese, his voice sounding to the rest of us like a beautiful kite's tail of gibberish, floating upward above us into the room, beguiling us, making us think it would all be this easy.

The Immortals:

Margot + Rudolf

4 Ever

1

In Pushkin's Leningrad apartment Rudi prowled, looking for food, one hand opening cupboards, the other stuffing crackers into his mouth. He was thirsty, too, and tense. Xenia slapped his hand away from the roast, on a plate under a tea towel. "Wait," she said. She would not look at him. Behind her at the table Pushkin was talking, reviewing the phrasing of the last bit of the solo from *Bayadère* that Rudolf would perform in Paris next week. "Rudi, remember, da da daa bam bam!" Rudi nodded; he had a chicken leg in his mouth. Pushkin shook his head. "Beast. Sit down. Be a bull on the stage. Here be a gentleman." Rudi sat. Xenia brought him a glass of tea and a glass of wine. He'd lived with them for almost three years, since his graduation from the Kirov school, where Pushkin had been his teacher. Now he was leaving, but here nothing was changed, same mahogany table, straight-backed chairs, the one bedroom where he slept next to the big bed on a narrow sofa.

Pushkin's wife was younger than Pushkin. She sat with them at the table, her chair turned sideways. She was pale, but she was always pale, her hair looped behind her ear. Rudi looked away. He adored Pushkin, and now forced his face to turn toward his teacher's, but his ears were not hearing what Pushkin was saying about the tour, the stage at the Garnier, the Albrecht he was to do opposite Alla Sizova's Giselle, the KGB security. Pushkin was offering him advice, but Rudi felt Xenia beside him, stirring possessively, her square shoulders wedged against the light from the window. Rudi finally interrupted Pushkin's gibberish, slapping his hand on the table and blurting out, "I've betrayed you," a remark which Pushkin was to think he understood only later, when news of Rudi's defection reached Russia.

2

The dry ice blew across the lake, powered by enormous fans set up in the fourth wings, stage right and stage left, grinding the mist out over the lakeshore, suggested by blue lights and a painted backdrop. The swans circled her, doing the bourrées with the occasional passé that made them look as if they were stepping out of the shallow water and shaking the drops off. Inside the circle she chaînéed, arms down in first, then up in fifth position, while on the outside hovered the prince, Michael Somes, booted, quiver of arrows on his back. The circle opened for him to behold her in her short white tutu, rhinestoned bodice, feathered headdress. He stepped toward her, knelt, and extended his arm in the opening motion of the pas de deux. After this, there were two more acts to go. She took his hand for the supported arabesque. She had been dancing *Swan Lake* for twenty years. She was Margot Fonteyn, prima ballerina assoluta of the Royal Ballet of England, and she was bored out of her mind.

3

He lingered at the grand magazine stand in St. Michel, beside the public rest room, watching the boys go in and come out, go in and come out. He had one more hour before he was due at the Avenue de l'Opéra for his first rehearsal in the West, and he stood, ten feet from the swinging black door. In Leningrad, with the KGB everywhere, the boys had been underground, quiet; no one in the company had known what he did in the private apartments of a few friends, a few times, that had left him sickened but still hungry. In the West the hunger could be appeased at any time, at any place, openly. The door swung, he went to it. He would be late for rehearsal.

4

I want to stay.

5

The room was crowded with diplomats and their wives in couture dresses, arms bare, eyes heavily made up in the fashion of the sixties. Margot worked one side of the room, Tito the other. Since his appointment as ambassador, they did this twice a week, when she was not at the theater. She saw him move through the opened doors to the terrace, his hand on the back of a blond woman. Margot held out her hand to the Brazilian attaché. When she'd first met Tito, at a party in the thirties in Cambridge, where the Wells was on tour, he was a twenty-year-old, black-haired Panamanian Adonis. But even then he had been at it, with one girl or another;

it was eighteen years before they met up again and were married, far too publicly to admit failure now.

6

He had, at Pushkin's apartment, watched a bootlegged film of Erik Bruhn dancing *Giselle*. Bruhn had been blond, long-legged, lean-muscled, and he had moved with a precision and elegance that became, instantly, Rudi's ideal, as he crouched there on Pushkin's floor, eyes focused on the living room wall that was the makeshift screen. Meeting Bruhn in Volkova's studio in Copenhagen, he saw that everything about him was long—long face, long chiseled features, long fingers, long limbs, and with that length came a remote quality, almost as if Bruhn were asleep. Rudi stood by him at the barre and then again in the first row center as they took class. They made the same movements: on Bruhn they were elegant, on Rudi robust. His legs were thicker, his muscles bulkier, his approach more athletic. He would never be Bruhn; all his training was wrong, and his character, and as he did a développé à la seconde and rotated carefully into arabesque, he looked into Bruhn's still face, saw something flicker behind Bruhn's cold eyes.

7

They did not get out of bed for two days. Rudi was fascinated by Bruhn, by his Nordic reserve, his cool passion, so cool that it burned, and Rudi rolled him into his fever until even Bruhn became sloe-eyed. When they left Bruhn's flat, it was Thursday, and they sat in a café in the Kongens Nytorv outside the Royal Theatre.

8

She had called him in Copenhagen, and now here he was, in London, in her studio, working his feet in the big square resin box, his broad legs made broader still by his heavy wool warmers. He wore a bandanna around his forehead. The Russian boy. Margot's reflection in the mirror fifteen feet away from him looked old, much older than his. She was forty-two, and the cords in her neck had begun to stand out. It was an embarrassment, but Rudolf Nureyev was the new curiosity; if she didn't dance with him, somebody else would. She stood there in her T-shirt and short white tutu, hair pinned. He finished at the resin box and looked up at her, at once shy and arrogant. He spoke little English, just enough to tell the French police, who had not understood him, *I want to stay.* The rehearsal pianist played the too familiar bars of Tchaikovsky, and Rudi stepped toward her, knelt, and extended his arm. She took it for the supported arabesque and looked in his face, which was charged with emotion, surprising her. When he stood and grasped her waist, then laid her over his arms for the backward lunge, again his face provoked her. His body was muscular where hers was delicate. Their arms and legs fell into a natural alignment at rest, and when raised, she saw that the Tatar bones of his face would contrast with her classical features, her dark hair. Together they rendered the familiar steps of the formal pas de deux mysteriously, and at first cautiously, erotic, and then, as the rehearsal progressed, more securely so. They were not alone in the studio; de Valois, the translator, pianist, ballet mistress, coach, and company photographer were also there, but it was the two of them and their bodies falling in love, the mutton and the lamb, it was unbelievable, and she thought at the last of it, *We will make a sensation.*

9

At the end of *Romeo and Juliet* they stood in the light, corpses raised and anointed by the ovation. Over the rails of the second balcony the fans had unrolled a banner, MARGOT + RUDOLF 4 EVER. The theater was shaking with whistles, feet stamping. They held hands at the center of it.

10

Bruhn was watching their performance of *La Sylphide* from the wings; Rudi had brought him to London for the season, and Bruhn had coached Rudi in this role famously his own. Bruhn stood backstage whenever Rudi danced, but when it was his turn, he would not have Rudi in the theater. The critics had turned the season into a competition. Each time Margot passed the third wing, burdened by her long, heavy tutu, the switch in her hair to thicken her coif, the pearls at her neck and wrists, she got a glimpse of him there, his hair as colorless and fine as floss, his drawn face. He looked miserable. Of course his James was the better James, truly Danish, truly Bournonville, with the purity of accent, the bounce. He had done everything right, everything beautifully, but for the fact that he had not defected from Russia and that he did not have on the stage a sexual presence. He was a danseur noble, not a superstar. As Rudi's partner, Margot had helped create his celebrity, but Bruhn would always be eclipsed by it. The stagehands secured the wire to the back of her costume, powered the crank. She took a few steps out of the wings and then began to float, a sylph. Rudi plowed the air by her, his arms making circles that embraced nothing, catching the edge of her tutu as she spun away.

11

Rudi had left Bruhn in the dressing room taking off his kilt from *Sylphide* and pulled the beige Mercedes convertible to the curb by the stage door to surprise him. Now he sat in the driver's seat, leather cap on his head, waiting to show off the latest of what Bruhn had come to call his movie star toys. When he emerged, Rudi almost leaped out of the car. He coveted Bruhn's attention; at home he would plead for it, cajole, demand, and Bruhn would draw back from him, his fingers working a cigarette, his legs shifting as he crossed and recrossed them. He did not have Rudi's appetite, and Rudi could not get enough of his love or of his flesh. He found himself resorting to the crying tantrums that had so bewildered his classmates back at the Kirov school, tantrums of which Pushkin had gradually cured him. Bruhn was as difficult as a knot of entrechats Rudi could not master, and the tensions of the London season had simply knotted him tighter. Rudi watched the stage door.

Bruhn paused, a blond god in his camel hair coat, to sign a few autographs, and then, as he spotted Rudi and strode toward the car, the fans turned with him, and soon a small crowd was thick around the Mercedes and growing thicker. By the time Rudi had finished with them all, Bruhn's face was cold and he would not speak. He took the cigarettes from his coat pocket and lit one, deliberately, and smoked it while Rudi drove away from the theater. The streets were long and dark, and Rudi felt them folding down around them in the little car, as if the buildings were cardboard playhouses unhatching at the seams and going flat. He wanted to take Bruhn's hand or touch his coat, but Bruhn kept his face turned to the passenger window. "I am, you know, the fucking quintessential James of our fucking generation." He would not look at Rudi, just breathed in the smoke that whirled around them both and then shot between them and over the back of the car. "This won't work. I'm going back to Copenhagen."

12

I burn everyone I touch, except you.

13

He paced his furnished flat, studded with thick, dark furniture, heavy velvet drapes at the windows, floor to ceiling. He stood at one of them and looked down at her car and driver. There was half the world between him and Erik. Between him and Margot there was Tito, in his Armani suits, with his graceful manners, unflappable and superior. Into the vacuum of Erik he had thrown his longing and his despair and they had risen back up to him in the shape of Margot. If Rudi had dared, he would have taken her tonight, up against the wall of the disco or by the back exit when the paparazzi had left, having finished their tabloid shots of the two of them on a busman's holiday—he on the strobe-lit floor in his leather pants and snakeskin boots, she in heels, black cocktail dress, and pearls. Her hair was in a chignon, but he knew what it looked like down, knew the shape of her lips, the smell of her breath and body, the feel of her bones. He had been with only a few women, and women did not usually stir him, they were inferior to men in brains and body, but Margot was different, was equal, and at the end of a ballet, he found it difficult to shake the desire they had consummated onstage. Her body had belonged to his and still should. She was running water in his bathroom, getting ready to leave. There was always this energy, this hunger. He took to the floor, alternating chaînés and wild barrel jetés in a large circle, his street clothes and the bangs of his hair drenched in the minute it took her to open the bathroom door. He stood there panting, opening and shutting his hands.

14

His legs and body in his tights and costume were white and sculptured, bedecked; his eyebrows and cheekbones were elaborately painted, his face savagely elegant, not Russian, but Tatar. Across the stage from him, she loved her lover; in the bed with him, shorn of his costume, all breath and hair, she loved him more.

15

Nureyev. Fonteyn. Ten minutes of *Le Corsaire*. Twenty minutes of applause.

16

She stooped in her *Corsaire* costume, tutu upended, the plume of her headdress scraping the ledge of his dressing table, which was littered with makeup. His leg warmers and shoes and tights were all over the place. They had a plane in two hours to Washington. He couldn't hear her through the shower asking about the white shoes. She put them in his satchel. His clothes were in piles, just like at home, and she began rolling the shirts. He refused a dresser and relied on her. She was overheated and hurried, and as she bent for his warmers she saw through the half-opened door the face of one of the company soloists; it wore an expression of embarrassment, and a sudden shame checked her mid-movement, Rudi's woolens in her arms.

17

A special floor had been laid over the parquet at the White House, and he was pounding it. The bounce of it gave him extra ballon, and his body, in jeté, hung in the air longer than was possible. He could see the impression it made on the faces of the American president and his family, the Johnsons, and their guests at the inaugural gala. Margot was irritated with him, he could feel it: there was an unusual brittleness in her body, and she would not meet his eyes. It might be the boys he had begun picking up on the side. Each time she faced him with her brilliant smile, she would look at his forehead or eyebrows. At the end of it they stood there in their sweat and their costumes, shaking hands with the president, the dignitaries. He was practically mute, his English was still no good, and he felt himself assume the arrogant posture that was his defense. Margot was so good at this, at ease with her weight on one leg, making the graceful pleasantries, she with all her diplomatic parties at the embassy. He strode off the stage to the little dressing area, hiding behind the myth of his Russian temper, and heard the murmur behind him that marked his exit, Was anything wrong? He would have double hell to pay. She hated to be upstaged. He took a thick wad of tissues and wiped at the makeup on his face. Well, fuck her, she could just dance harder. He was Rudolf Nureyev—she was dancing with him, he was not serving her. But she would have none of it when she joined him at the back of the stage. "I saw your book.

You've got engagements from Australia to America next year. There's not a bit of you left for London."

So that was it. He put down the wipes. "I have to go."

"I have, maybe, five years left."

"You come with me."

He stood there, arms crossed, doing as he did on the stage where they danced in both partnership and competition, each afraid the one might grab the light from the other. She gazed at him, impassive, the long wings of eyeliner angling upward away from her eyes. He smiled. She would go.

18

The full-length *Firebird* was a bit beyond her at age forty-four, but she had plowed through it, energized in part by Rudolf's glee that she was with him here, in Melbourne, on the raked stage, which she hated, but which he was used to, of course, from Russia. Now she stood in the wings, in her red feathered costume, pacing. The houselights were to half, intermission over, but Rudi could not be found. He had vanished after the first act, slipped out the stage door already crowded with their fans, the souvenir programs held up like machetes. She knew what he was off doing. It had gotten so she would not enter his dressing room without knocking and waiting. He would bring the boys there, but off on tour he went out for them. They held the curtain five minutes, ten. The audience had begun its chant, "We want Rudi," even as his understudy had begun to warm up. The fans wanted them both—the sum of the two of them greater than either of them alone—and the booking agent had gotten them top dollar, which might now have to be repaid. She worked her feet in their pointe shoes. When Rudi arrived, finally, grandly, back-stage, intermission had stretched to forty-five minutes. He was still wearing the broad fur hat, his tights, his entire *Firebird* cos-tume, in fact, covered only partially by the long cloak she had bought him in London a few years ago after their triumph as Romeo and Juliet.

19

In Bath they received the news. Tito had been gunned down in Panama.

20

The press was told it had been an assassination attempt related to his diplomatic post that paralyzed him, not that Tito had been shot by a cuckolded husband. Margot took the salve, rolled him to the bed, opened his dressing gown. His middle had thickened and his legs had shriveled. Under her hands she felt his flesh go smooth. The side of his abdomen held a knot of scar tissue, and the left leg was stiff, as if the muscles and tendons, even the skin, had dried into strips of jerky. She turned him over. His thighs and back had no sores. When she was finished, she lay on top of him, her cheek at the nape of his neck, inhaling the scent of the salve, the rinse he had used on his hair. He would go nowhere now.

21

She sat between Tito in his chair and Rudi in the metal garden one. The night-blooming primrose made a mist all around them. It was August, preautumnal, and cool.

22

He began to tour constantly, with a few months left for London and Margot. Glasgow. Amsterdam. Vienna. Zurich. Lausanne. Basel. Geneva. The Hague. New York. Paris. London. New York. Paris. He had bought another apartment, this one in New York, and in the living room he had put the bed, a massive four-columned thing with a roof like a medieval church. And he hid from her in it, on his knees, bent over the body of a boy. The boy was groaning, the muscles in his arms were tensed against the dancer's weight, his fists on the mattress. Rudi needed this, the miraculous energy it provided, which he had first discovered back in Russia, in his dressing room with Xenia. But women were so much work, and with Margot there were so many complications. With boys it was quick, big explosion, then great clarity. By tonight, he would be out cruising again.

23

"Rudi found it easier this way," she said, adjusting his hands at her waist. "Then bend beneath and up." They worked through the passage again, Act II, *Giselle*. Her face reassumed its sorrowful expression, and David Blair worked steadily behind her, dutifully pumping her up and down, up and down, in the long series of lifts from backstage right to upstage left.

24

"You stand here," Ashton demonstrated, "and when Margot presents the flowers to you, you spurn them, toss them at her." He jerked his arm. "It will be a public humiliation for her. This is at the party. You don't know she's been ill." They ran it through, the scene from *Marguerite and Armand,* Rudi drawing himself up to his full height, dashing the flowers at her, nostrils spread with the pain of his misreading of her. Margot looked older to him, her hair partially pinned up, the long, soft tutu poufing about her as she sank to her knees. She looked older and then she looked younger, as they marked the adagio. She was mercurial, a theatrical genius. He adored her, even as she clipped him, she was always chip, chip, chipping away at him, trying to make him her houseboy, but he could not stop the boys and she would not end her marriage. She moved lithely. He stalked her round and round the studio, his body longer than hers, twisting this arm of hers and then the other, until he bent her, finally, almost to the floor, making her submit, humiliating her for what was clearly her love for him, until Ashton said, "Good. Good enough."

25

He sat on the ledge in one of the downtown baths, towel furled across his groin, until a blond boy, thin and tall like Bruhn, came and knelt before him and put his hands and then his head beneath the towel. The boy's back looked like Bruhn's, the sharp planes of his ass. But it wasn't Bruhn. None of the boys was ever Bruhn. Bruhn never frequented the bars or baths Rudi compulsively haunted, enjoying the recognition, the theatricality of the public act. Rudi and the boy had drawn a crowd as Rudolf was recognized, *it's Nureyev!* Rudi pushed the towel off and stood to let the others watch the boy work. Bruhn could hide. Let them all watch Nureyev. Yes, he was Nureyev, sour with flesh.

26

It was during *Don Q.* in Madrid. The ballerina of the evening had grazed his eye with her fan, then refused to plié in preparation for the grand lifts, forcing him to raise her like a barbell. She was tiny and compact, a principal from the national company, but heavy as a lump from a neutron star. He refused to return to the stage for the final coda, leaving her to dance the frantic allegro herself; he watched from the wings as she improvised during the dead spots made by his absence. And when she strode across the stage to him at the curtain, he stared down her fury, made the slap at her face that caused a tempest.

27

He was a pig in rehearsal, of course she knew that, she was not a fool, she had not gotten where she had gotten by being a fool. But he knew she would endure it. Freddie Ashton had worked on her feet, *Margot's little pats of butter,* had shown her all the carry-on Pavlova made with her hands and eyes to such great effect, but it was Rudi, with the Russian training that so intimidated Freddie, who had given her what she had never had—jump, attack, precision in her beats—as well as the partnership that had brought her immortality. Dancing with him she now truly embodied her great title, prima ballerina assoluta, carried before her by Taglioni

and Pavlova and Kschessinskaya and Ulanova, by only a handful
of ballerinas. In the studio he would attack her, sneer at her,
shout, stamp, but she would remain implacable Margot, turning
away to the resin box if he had gone too far. He never walked out.
He needed her, too. Without her to partner, de Valois would have
less use for him, and he would be shed. She ground the shanks
and pointes of her Freeds in the box, until the dark pebbles of
resin were yellow dust.

28

They danced Ashton's *Birthday Offering,* her tutu and his vest em-
bellished with stripes and ruffles and pompoms. They were of-
ferings themselves, a gift of the two ballet bloodlines converging:
the classicism and purity that characterized the English ballet, the
strength and bravura of the Russian. Margot was all grace and
graciousness, and tonight he followed her lead. When the houselights went up they stood side by side. He turned to Margot and
kneeled. She put her hand on his shoulder and the house went
quiet.

29

It was early morning and he was alone at barre, in his woolens
held up by suspenders, doing pliés in the absolute silence of the
studio. This was his routine, each day without exception. No
matter how late he went to bed, he was here, by 10:00. He stared
at the mirror without admiration, checking the knees, the line
of the back, the port de bras. The resin on his shoes helped him
hold the exaggerated turnout he favored as he moved steadily

through the exercises. He sloughed the woolens as he grew warmer, clipped the suspenders to his tights, continued the private watch. He would keep on without her. He was not just tea cozy for teapot.

30

The stage was dark with just the yellow spot. Ashton had made a short dance for her, the last of a long strand of dances short and long, and it contained small signature moments from each—she was Juliet, Marguerite, Ondine in turn. The final gesture had brought one arm down to frame the head, a quicksilver movement that made her look, for that moment, sixteen instead of sixty: her final gift to the world of balletomanes so reluctant, after five decades, to see her go.

31

His body was stone and his costume tight, the jacket and vest of Prince Albrecht. He had thickened after thirty, and he had begun to lose his strength, then his jump, his speed, and finally his clarity of movement, particularly in allegro. As he rounded the stage in a series of jetés (once barrel jetés and now simply jetés with the occasional chaîné in between), he felt his face tighten with the effort of launching his body time after time from the floor to the air, which had become thick and impregnable, like wax. At forty-nine, Margot had still been dancing *Giselle* with him, a floating, weightless Wili. At the time he thought, Of course she can do it, she's a great dancer. Now he thought she must truly have been an ageless creature from another world. At the finish he stood, panting for breath, one arm sweeping from left to right to accept the applause, struggling for the half grin that made the lie: This was easy.

32

After two years of negotiations, he was artistic director of the Paris Opéra. He would not spend more than six consecutive months in Paris, he would perform forty times a year and on all opening nights, they would build him three new studios, he would mount his own productions. The Opéra reminded him of home, with the bureaucratic machinery and the funding of the state, and in Paris there were so many boys. He took an apartment near the Avenue de l'Opéra, where he could see the Garnier from his bedroom. He used the place like a warehouse—the kilims he collected he stacked under the bed and on the floors of the closets, the paintings were framed but not hung, and leaned three thick against the walls. He piled silver on the buffet. A large TV screen stood in the dining room, and from his baroque table he watched every channel, switching from one to the other late into the night, looking at what else the world had to offer him.

33

Sylvie's movements unfolded as he coached her now in his third season at the Opéra. He had promoted her from corps de ballet to étoile in one year. She stood solidly on one leg in the center, the other raised in développé, the leg so high her thigh almost brushed her ear. Her arms were not even at her sides for balance, but in the air in fifth. Unbelievably, effortlessly, she made a slow relevé from the flat of her foot to the ball. She was an incredible technician, too young yet to be a great artist, but she would grow under his tutelege. He would partner her himself in *Swan Lake*. The Opéra audience had begun to boo him when he appeared on the stage, but with her there they would not. She would breathe life into his age, as he had for Margot. He had begun, ridiculously, to buy her gifts. She put her leg down and stood before him sweating in her unitard, the zippered front of it open to her sternum, her hair colored a coppery red. He drank coffee as they took their break. She named cities to him in her French-accented English, an accent almost as thick as his Russian one: Madrid, Zurich, London, New York, cities he had trekked through over and over and had exhausted, and she was going to her big leather bag to show him her engagement book, a black thing held closed with a rubber band.

34

Margot watched from the front as he strode, lionlike, across the stage and then turned to face them all, dressed in one of the elaborate costumes he had had especially tailored. His face was the face she had looked at across the stage for fifteen years: the beautiful Tatar cheekbones, the blackened eyebrows, the impassioned hauteur. When he began his variation, she did not see the inelastic jump or the blurred beats or the uncertain balance. She saw Nureyev.

35

Will you love me.
Yes.
Will you love me always?
Yes.

36

He could see in the faces of his dancers that he was about to lose his temper. They feared him and watched him closely, were keenly reactive. Beneath the knit cap he wore when he rehearsed, his nostrils must have flared and his lips pursed. He was capable of throwing things, water bottle, coffee thermos, those Italian mints, Tic Tacs. He walked up and down the rows of girls, grappling with the impatience he always felt when working with an inferior artist, which was almost everybody except for Margot, Bruhn, Sylvie, and a few others. How many like him were there in this world? He struggled first in French and then in English, both the languages heavily plastered with the accent that drove all words to their knees, and then began to demonstrate with his body and arms how the long, shifting rows were to cross in the vision scene from *Sleeping Beauty*. He used the body of one girl, moving her arms roughly, one hand at her back. "Do, do." He resumed his position at the front before them, back to the mirror, crossed his arms. They began again, these young girls of eighteen, nineteen, limbs trembling with exhaustion and anxiety at their proximity to the ferocious legend.

37

The BBC crew had come to Panama to film her in retirement; she pushed Tito, and the cameras strolled ahead and behind them, panning the acreage of their ranch, deeply indebted. Where the garden sloped down to a field were the boxes that held the horses they bred and trained, one source of income. But even that and Tito's pension and all the liens could not much longer hold them and this place together. She had danced ten years longer than she should have, but Tito's medical bills were still astronomical. Now he was dying, and the estate would be foreclosed on. But all this would be beyond the camera's ken. The horses were brought out, a black one and a roan, and they were made to run around the track. Tea was laid outdoors. The final images of Dame Margot would be as staged a presentation as had been her art.

38

This body cannot be ill.

39

The Russian Tea Room in New York City, stage set of the motherland: red velvet, black rye, caviar, balalaikas. Rudi sat on the thick-cushioned, tassled banquette beside the trio—Valery Panov, Mikhail Baryshnikov, Alexander Godunov. He shared with them the journey away from Russia, but these boys he had shared a country with still had years to go in their beautiful bodies. His own body, once the vital casing into which he had funneled his best self, was a husk. This would soon be visible to all. It would shrivel, shrink, and, at the pull of a string, split in two. He drank vodka with his fellows, poured the stuff into the hole of his mouth. Montmartre Cemetery. Père-Lachaise. Sainte-Geneviève-des-Bois. There. In that one. With a Romanov, with Prince Felix Yussupov, with Trefilova, Kschessinskaya, Preobrajenska, with all the White Russians in exile.

40

In the Toronto hospital Bruhn lay quietly on the narrow bed as if afraid to rouse the three-headed tumor of his lung cancer. Rudi sat on the window ledge, allowed to remain in deference to their former intimacy, while the nurse bathed Bruhn; she lifted first one limb and then the next, squeezing the sponge into a ball, permitting only the water to touch the skin. Rudi spoke. "In the papers they write that I should retire. I'm fat, I'm weak. 'Where is Nureyev?' They want me twenty years old. Or not at all." Bruhn smiled. His face looked much the same, though thinner and pale. "It's their revenge, Rudi, to humble you. Unrequited desire is a terrible thing." The nurse finished, and Rudi moved to the chair by the bed. "I miss it," Bruhn said. Rudi took his hand. "Even now," said Bruhn. "Even now, I feel desire."

41

He walked through the park, leather cap covering his thinning hair. He was fifty-three, and the boys walked past him, passed him by.

42

The Royal Ballet staged a benefit, proceeds to defray the medical expenses of Dame Margot Fonteyn, now seriously ill.

43

He had brought to her in Panama a Dior dressing gown, impossibly frilled, a joke, and it had made her laugh her famous trilling laugh when it presented itself, after the symphony of ribbons and tissue paper. Of course he should have brought her money, but he sat on his money, he always sat on his money, he couldn't share, not even with her; he was for himself and he knew she knew it, had always known it; it was that, not the boys, not Tito, that had kept her from him. Margot shook out the big balloon of a gown, and through its many filmy layers, he saw her, not as she was now, seventy and sick with cancer in her run-down ranch house in Panama, ninety-five degrees in the bedroom with the shutters closed, the nurse waiting in the hall with the morphine. No, she was Juliet, the girl with the long, dark hair and the white gown over her white tights who had stood with him in 1966 before the grand bed on the great stage at Covent Garden.

44

Under the morphine, it was 1928 and she was Peggy Hookham, age fourteen, with blue-black hair, at the end of the long row of girls at the barre, and de Valois was an English lady in heels, leaning forward to peer at her, asking of Madame, Who is the little Chinese girl in the corner?

45

They lifted the chaise and bore him onto the stage at the end of
the calls for *Bayadère*. He reclined, legs crossed at the calves, turban on his head, the dying *roi*. He stared into the faces of his
Opéra dancers and into the face of the audience and let them stare
back at his own unnerving visage. His dancers, some in the long,
white tutus from the "Kingdom of the Shades," Act II, some in
the jeweled saris and pantaloons from the "The Temple," Act III,
stood applauding him. The audience also stood, in the rhythmic
stamp and clap that made the Garnier vibrate. He would, in a
moment, receive the medal of a Commander of Arts and Letters
from the French Minister of Culture. And they were all there—
Dupond, Grigorovich, MacMillan, even Sylvie Guillem. Now
that he was unable to dance, was able only to provoke the
memory of his dancing, they would all embrace him.

46

It was his mother, bringing him paper with cows drawn on it and
colored pencils to fill in the shapes. It was cold. She turned the
dial on the radio, sharpened the red, showed him the mark it
could make on a paper. They were in Ufa, in the Ural province
of Bashkiria, in the center of an Asian Russian landscape so vast,
so rugged, it astonished him that it had yielded the five sweet-
colored pencils.

47

Fonteyn was gone.

48

He woke alone in his overheated quai Voltaire apartment, body drenched, a boat capsized at sea; he got up and stood before the music stand in the living room, turning over the pages of the score to the Bluebird variation, the boy's solo, from *Sleeping Beauty*. It was a tank of a variation; he was too sick with the plague to dance it anymore. He and Soloviev had been coached by Pushkin for this role for graduation performance; Soloviev had gone on to join the company, but Rudi had stayed back, at Pushkin's suggestion, to repeat his ninth year. After regular class, Pushkin remained behind with him, and they would water the big studio floor themselves before rehearsing all the male variations in classical ballet. Rudolf had come to ballet late, at fifteen, and everything had frustrated him, but now he was an encyclopedia, he knew it all—*Beauty, Bayadère, Giselle, Swan Lake, Corsaire, Paquita, Don Quixote, Sylphide, Raymonda.* Alone with Pushkin he had been all kinds of princes, hunters, and cavaliers, and he had learned to be strong, to be imperial, to command. He had carried that knowledge with him when he left Russia, and he had used it to conquer the West. But now he was in a new hemisphere, and it could not be conquered. To this hemisphere he must submit, without knowing the steps or where they would take him. The ballets he had given his life to had not taught him how to be ill or to age or to die.

Prince of Desire

$\mathcal{J}$ames sat woozily at the kitchen table, getting a buzz from his sister's cigarette smoke, which pooled above them in an oily nicotine cloud. Joanna puffed as she flipped through the fat layout of herself in *Bazaar* magazine. Photographed in her costume first for *Bugaku* and then for *Sleeping Beauty,* she seemed unreal, a superhuman, superglossy vision. The white seamed tights zipped her endless legs up and into the petaled bikini and then the feathered and jeweled tutu. The actual Joanna looked somewhat less vivid without the costumes and the Pan-Cake and the lashes and the klieg lights, but beautiful still, more beautiful, to him. This Joanna held a heating pad to her knee, the black extension cord running up over the magazine and the toaster oven to the wall outlet.

By weird coincidence, both the New York City Ballet and the San Diego Ballet were staging *Sleeping Beauty* this season. Not that anybody in New York knew this, of course, or knew anything about what was going on in podunk San Diego, except Joanna. She had flown out to California to see him open, tomorrow night.

James looked beyond her to the dark shape of the pool out

back. His place was a piece of shit, a beach shack, but it had this. The night lights clipped thin yellow scallops to the surface of the water. He could almost see his wife's body out there, in the water, long hair floating, her enormous swimmer's rib cage gouging out the center of the pool. She wasn't there. She wasn't anywhere in the house. He looked away from the pool.

"So who's your Prince Florimund?" James asked Joanna.

"Damian Woetzel. Wish it were you."

"I'm already somebody's prince."

"Not anymore, baby. Not in real life."

"Thanks, Joanna. I forgot about that for, like, one millisecond."

Joanna laughed. She and Ellen hadn't ever gotten along well.

"I should have married a dancer," James said.

"They have their own personalities, too, you know," Joanna said wryly. She'd been married to two of them.

"Well, Ellen couldn't stand mine."

"What Ellen couldn't stand," Joanna said, "was that you had real talent. What was she going to do with her swimming, paddle around all day at the Y?"

"She could have gone to the Olympics," James said.

"Jamie, the girl was cut from the team at State."

"She quit, she wasn't cut." He couldn't help himself. But the truth was, if she hadn't quit, she would have been cut.

"Okay, James," Joanna said. "Fine." She put her cigarette up to her lips, superior and insouciant, and for a minute James hated her. "Look," she said, "I brought you something for merde," and she sank her hand into one of her robe's deep pockets, lifted out a chain with a cross soldered to it. Great. The walls of Joanna's minuscule apartment in New York were crammed with the crucifixes she'd collected, as if she could never collect for herself enough merde, enough luck. When James had stayed with her last year for his New York City Ballet audition, he'd slept beneath a huge iron monstrosity that had pressed itself, swastika-like, into his dreams. New York had given him nightmares. Looking at that memory was like staring at the pulverized flecks of color at the far end of a kaleidoscope.

"Hey, baby," Patty said, as he neared her. She was pacing in the corridor by the battered studio door, a long pair of woolen tights twisted several times about her neck, the baggy knees dangling against her breasts. "Kiss me."

James put his head close and smelled the hard odor of 4711, the German spray cologne Patty used all over her body and re-hearsal clothes, even though he had told her he hated it. Clutch-ing her in one of the famous upside-down fish dives from the final *Sleeping Beauty* pas de deux, he'd find himself sneezing, knocking her hard against his sternum in that awkward, bent-over position. Patty would put a hand down on the floor and laugh. She had long, fine hair, the same reddish color as his wife's, but her body was entirely different, much narrower and lighter, the musculature longer, less intense. James had taken Patty out a few times since Ellen left him.

"Your sister's already in there. I'm not going in until after the barre," Patty whispered as James opened the door. He made a sign at her and shut the door between them. He'd surfed too long this morning. He wasn't very late, though it wouldn't matter if he had been. He was everybody's baby in the company, a rarity in Southern California, a good male dancer. He took his place at the barre, right behind Joanna, and started to work, trying to catch up, doing the familiar repetitive motions.

In front of him, Joanna was already deep into her barre, doing her développés, the long, strong muscles of her legs and the powerful arches of her feet as arresting as her absolute control. Nobody else in the room could touch her. She'd left San Diego at fourteen, quit high school and moved to New York to cut her way through the vicious competition at the School of American Ballet. She had to, if she wanted a shot at the company: she was a girl, girls in pink tights were a dime a dozen. James, however, had the luxury of kicking around the San Diego public school system seemingly forever, doing his dancing on the side. But when Joanna came back to visit and took class at his studio, James saw the payoff—in her technique, her panache. She had turned herself into a racehorse, and he was nothing but a pokey-ass donkey. She'd been a star to him long before she really was a star.

At the break, James pulled on some scraggly tan leg warmers and paced. He couldn't take the fifteen minutes between class and rehearsal, couldn't stand to smoke or fart around. He put some quarters in the hall vendor and downed a Tab, and when he went back into the studio, he looked for Patty, spotted her against the back barre with a klatch of girls around Joanna. Every time Joanna came to town, it took about a week for the company girls to copy everything about her, from the latest New York trends in practice clothes to the way she put up her hair. She was a blonde, but you'd never know it. Balanchine didn't like blondes on the stage, thought the bright lights blanched them until they looked bald up there in their tutus. So Joanna had turned herself into a brunette. Living in New York had made her pale, too, and she and James had never looked more unalike—the sun stripped his hair lighter than hers had ever been and deepened his skin to the point where he used only black liner and rouge for the stage. He looked more like a fucking lifeguard than a dancer. James, nearing the girls at the barre, heard Patty saying to Joanna, "I saw you in New York last winter. You were awesome." Patty's face flushed, and James, watching, saw that Joanna made her nervous. Patty picked her pointe shoes off her rehearsal tutu and put them over her hands like two puppets. "I saw you in *Bugaku* and *Symphony in C*. What's it like dancing with Damian Woetzel?"

James turned away. Fuck Damian Woetzel.

The rehearsal pianist played a few bars of the grand adagio from Act III, the wedding adagio. They were working on that first. Patty walked toward him. She'd put on her hard pointe shoes and her woolen tights. He could see the liner around her eyes. She'd made herself up, pinned her hair into a French twist. There was color on her lips. She held out her hand, and he led her in a big circle from the dull ambulation into the sweeping opening postures of the showcase pas de deux. James found himself superaware of Joanna, almost as if he were dancing with her instead of Patty, his mind on her and not the body in front of him, until he pivoted out from Patty's shadow for a moment and saw in Joanna's eyes excitement, approval. That released him, that and Patty's pelvic bone smacking against his hipbone as he levered her into a slanted arabesque, the length of her tight to the length of him. She was gripping his forearms, thumbs pitted deep into the sides of his elbows. "Quit sweating on me," she whispered, as he set her upright. He balanced her like a top. The two of them were partners of several years, and they knew each other's bodies as well as two people could. So many movements were by now for them mechanical that there was no thinking about where their hands or legs went or how to balance this attitude or that turn. He knew what she could and could not do, where she needed support and where he could release her, how to touch her and exactly how she felt. Dancing with her, in fact, was the closest thing James had known to a marriage in months.

He had his wet suit half on, the arms and trunk of it peeled down and flapping against his thighs as he rhythmically waxed his board, his best board, the long board. Without Ellen, he still surfed every morning in the gray predawn, though the water now seemed empty and pale. They used to walk the half block to the beach together, boards tucked under their arms like purses. They both swam varsity, but she was a powerhouse. James used to stay late to watch the women's team practice even before he knew her, just to see her plowing down her lane a half body ahead of the other women, smacking the water up against the rope and floats with the force of her butterfly. In bed he'd beg her to flex her muscles, and the two of them would fuck for hours in the little room by her parents' garage. He loved the look of her, with her straight-edged nose, her long, fine fingers, the fingers of a surgeon, the broad back, and the smell of her, too, sometimes like salt, sometimes like chlorine. They had married senior year when they turned eighteen, and that had made them celebrities at La Jolla High. The two athletes, mated. But Ellen was, of the two of them, supreme: focused, disciplined, accomplished. She'd have taken the New York City Ballet contract.

"Nervous?" Joanna was standing at the sliding glass door to the pool.

James nodded, put a hand to his stomach. He got the runs before every performance. "I'm gonna fuck up tonight."

"No, you won't. You'll do great. Just like in New York."

James couldn't look at her. She was going to start in on him

again. He remembered the sensation of that audition. His goddamn nerves, all those gorgeous dancers, the way he nailed company class, every move going right, vaulting through the air,
pounding the boards. He'd been offered a contract before he'd
gotten his breath back. But when he flew home to California and
told Ellen, he knew immediately the whole audition thing had
been a big mistake, not what he had expected. He had done it to
woo her, their marriage was crumbling, already, within a year,
but she wasn't wooed. She was jealous. He hadn't been able to
paddle away from it all fast enough. That night, when he tried
to do her, she lay beneath him like something beached and too
heavy to push back into the surf.

He looked up at his sister at the sliding glass door. "I had to
turn it down, Joanna."

"She left anyway."

"I don't blame her," James said.

"Look," Joanna said. "You wanted to dance with City Ballet.
Do you have to punish yourself for that? Make yourself stay here
forever?" She came and sat beside him, and she smoked half a
cigarette before she spoke again. "You're a pretty big fish here,
Jamie. Maybe you've gotten to like that just a little too much."

"Ashamed of me, big ballerina?" He moved his body away in
its wet suit, tucked the bottom of the board to his feet.

Joanna looked over at him. "*You* asked *me* to arrange the audition, James."

"I know, I know." He put his head down.

They'd all been so good in company class. It was like dancing with a chorus of gods. He'd had a good day, but he knew he
didn't always dance that well. It wasn't only because of Ellen that
he'd turned down the contract. He was uncertain of his technique, uncomfortably challenged. And there'd be no surfing

there, no skipping class, no letup ever. He just wasn't sure he was up to it. He knew he was undisciplined, a fuckup with a gift. That was partly what had driven Ellen nuts. She had put in the hours at the pool, and he was a kid who'd followed his sister into ballet class just for the hell of it.

James gripped his board, feeling suddenly a sickening echo of the theatrical hunger he'd portrayed yesterday in dress rehearsal. He'd stood alone in the forest of Act II, having sent away the hunting party, a solitary figure before a backdrop thick with trees. He was a prince longing for love, full of desire. It had been an immense moment on the stage, his loneliness almost physically painful, like a pressure, until the lights came down.

Behind the curtain they could feel the enormous, animal-like vibration coming from the body of the audience. Things had gone well. Patty put her foot down for a moment and then shot it back up as the curtain rolled away so it would appear as if they had all been frozen for that hidden period in their final, triumphant postures. The curtain down, he and Patty and the other featured dancers scrambled to the wings so the corps could take their call. Patty took hold of him for balance, checked her ribbons, her paste-and-glitter tiara, and then stood, panting, beside him, watching the corps. He had nothing to check.

"Come here," Patty said suddenly, grabbing his jaw, and the two of them stood kissing there in the wing, the thick black material hanging in scrolls all around, partially obscuring them. Beyond them was the stage full of movement. He had his hands on her neck, and the flesh of her shoulders and breasts was salty. She clutched at his head, his chain with Joanna's crucifix, letting him do whatever he wanted, but he made himself stop. He didn't want a hard-on for their curtain call. Patty laughed at him, both of them goofy and high. There was a roll of applause, and Patty turned to look at the stage, at the dancers taking their reward. "We should be dancing in New York," she said, without looking at him. "You know that? The company stinks."

James put a hand through his hair.

"We should be dancing at Lincoln fucking Center," Patty said, slicing her eyes to him and away.

James didn't look up. Patty was an okay dancer, good enough for San Diego, but she couldn't cut it in New York. She wouldn't even be able to get a corps contract there. They were partners here, equals here, but he knew what she couldn't do and what he could.

"I need a drink," Patty said. "Let's get this thing over with and go party."

She took his hand and shuffled him over behind her: their call was next. He could see the muscles in her back ripple as she prepared herself. For what? From his oblique angle in the first wing, James could see the red exit light over the side door of the rented college auditorium in which he and the company had performed.

It was a quarter to one when James finally rolled through the front door, finished with Patty. Making it with her had been like making it with some punctured and partially deflated version of Ellen, same reddish hair by his face, but nothing else at all the same, and he was exhausted. The house was quiet, almost entirely dark, but James spied Joanna on the back patio, the cord of the phone running a line from the dining room wall out the sliding glass doors and into the black. He could just barely see the shape of her. James put down his bag and stood still, listening. She was probably talking to New York, to some amphetamine-high insomniac who'd finished a performance four hours ago and still couldn't slow down. He could hear her laughing, the flutter of words, the nicknames of famous dancers and ballets from the New York City Ballet repertoire. *Stars and Stripes.* Merrill Ashley. *Calcium Light Night.* Darci and Peter. Suzanne. Ridley, her boyfriend of ten years ago who was retiring this season. It was all Joanna knew. It was her whole life, all there was to it. She'd lived year after year in a series of cheap apartments, and when each of her marriages broke up she'd acted less upset than when she was dumped as the lead in a Jerome Robbins ballet. It had been James's habit to scoff at her, but perhaps he had simply feared her, feared the sister of that ambition within himself.

Joanna put down the phone and waved at him, and James opened the sliding glass door. She was wearing one of Ellen's old swimsuits, a dark blue, and it looked wet. He was surprised she'd been able to find it. The day Ellen quit the team at State, she had zoomed around the house gathering up all her swimming paraphernalia, her goggles and Speedos and earplugs, even her wet suit, and driven the load to the Dumpster on Seventh Street. Then she went out and registered for seventeen credits of mechanical engineering, a ridiculous load, and wouldn't let James mention water or swimming again. The cult of the body was over and with it, though James hadn't realized it at the time, the marriage.

James sat down by Joanna on the slate. The pool lights were off, the water thick.

"So what does being divorced feel like?" James asked.

"You tell me," Joanna said.

"I'm not divorced yet."

"It feels bad," Joanna said, after a pause. "What do you think? But there are compensations."

"Bugaku? Symphony in C?"

"Yes," Joanna said. *"Bugaku. Symphony in C. Sleeping Beauty."*

She took his wrist and pulled him up, moving, before he understood what she was doing, into the center of the big adagio he had just finished two hours ago with Patty. She was like something else, though, in his arms, the whole dance goosed up ten notches. Joanna's extensions were higher than Patty's, her body more pliant. Her assured carving out of the steps and the certainty of her balance liberated him, helping him to conserve his strength, and he found it an easy thrust when lifting her straight-armed to the sky. Her one leg extended directly up, the sharp plane of her back cut through horizontal space, her arms framed fearlessly beyond the slope of her neck. She was a black shape stuck against the stars until he peeled her away from them and put her back on the ground, where he matched her step for step, flourish for flourish, until she turned from him suddenly and, without a word, jumped into the pool. In the water, she was a shadow more than a shape. It took only a moment before he dove into the water in his clothes to follow her, as he had always followed her, the dark mark of her just ahead of him, full of grace.

The Brahmins

I don't think I ever would have moved to Los Angeles if I hadn't just quit the ballet and broken up with my boyfriend, Jack. Simultaneously. I was mooning around New York, working as a nanny for my sister Alison and basically driving her crazy, when one day I videotaped my five-year-old niece Katie at her peewee ballet class. The girls were so serious and so absurdly dressed in diminutive tutus and studded tiaras (as if they were miniature ballerinas rather than spastic five-year-olds) that I wound up using the whole cassette. Dancing was still bliss to them, and when they looked in the mirror all they saw were beautiful princesses. They hadn't learned any different yet. I went back with Peter's old camera again and again, and pretty soon Alison suggested I make a 16 mm about ballet students and let her show it to a friend of hers in the industry. I liked the idea, but I didn't want to go haunting ballet schools in New York, where everybody knew me as this ex–corps de ballet failure. So that's how it came about that I was running around the City of Angels with Alison's insurance money in my pocket, scoping out ballet schools in the September heat and trying to shoot my footage of ballet girls.

But today was a bad day, a day when the city convulsed with filmmakers and all the good camera equipment was checked out at Hollywood Cinema. And even though I stamped my feet and made a fuss and hissed at the clerk at the rental counter, there was no way I was going to get the camera and cables I needed to shoot my twelve-year-old girls at the Center for the Dance. I'd already filmed them in the dressing room, and today I was supposed to film them at the barre. But instead, I had to climb down off the loading dock empty-handed. I was so pissed I decided to bag going to Clifton's Cafeteria, where I sometimes washed dishes to make a few extra bucks, and instead I decided to take what reels I had over to Mona's. She's the editor on my film. I'd met her at one of those indie screenings, where cubes of Velveeta cheese are set out amid toothpicks and plastic cups and lots of twenty-somethings stand around in black attire talking cinema. It was also at one of those parties where I met my new boyfriend, Denny. But that's another California story, so hold on a minute.

First I had to stop at home to get my reels. Our little half bunga-low was dense with heat, but nonetheless Denny was bound up in the flannel bathrobe and raglan socks that constitute his writing outfit. But he wasn't writing. He was talking on the phone with my address book spread open before him. When I stepped into the living room, he hurriedly and furtively put down the phone. Something about it all—the way he was hunched over, the furtiveness, my address book splayed open—made me suspicious, and then certain.

"You called my contacts!" I said.

"Ka-tie." He stood up, wrung his hands. "I had to do it, Katie."

I went shrieking down the narrow hall to the bedroom with Denny coming after me, going "Ka-tie, Ka-tie," in this singsong voice I hate. Ever since Denny'd moved in with me, we'd been wrangling over these "contacts," which constituted a few names that a friend of Alison's had given me, with the idea that I could call them for a job or whatever it is you call contacts for, but Denny wanted me to let him use them. I'd always refused, thinking I might need them for myself someday.

"I can't believe you just went into my personal address book without permission and called those people up! Now I can never call them. Did you mention my name?"

"I might have."

"I hate you!"

"Ka-tie, I thought it might help my script! I wanted to help my script!"

"Ha!" I threw my stuff down on the bed. "You went into my personal things! That's like reading somebody else's mail. It's worse!"

"I had to do it for my script!"

His script.

While I was off all day shooting footage of my ballet girls, Denny was hunched over the desk in the bedroom of our ticky-tacky Hollywood bungalow chewing on long strips of paper he'd pull out of a spiral notebook while he typed maniacally onto fresh bond the revised draft of his screenplay. An autobiographical script about his divorced parents, it had been rejected by producers and festivals all across the United States, but by the time the script was rejected by one place, a different script had emerged from the typewriter to be sent on to the next. It was in a constant state of mutation and metamorphosis. As was our relationship. But Denny was talking again. "There're two kinds of people in this world, Katie: the Brahmins and the Untouchables. And we're the Untouchables! We don't know anybody, we don't meet the moguls at parties. We've got to do it on our own, any way we can."

We were all Untouchables here in the flats at the foot of the Hollywood Hills. In fact, come to think of it, that's what I'd been even in the flats of Manhattan. An Untouchable upstage, stage left, stage right, anywhere but center stage.

"So what did the Brahmins say to you?" I asked Denny.

"I don't think they really wanted to talk to me," he said. "They didn't seem that interested in my film."

No wonder.

When I'd met Denny two months ago, he had lumbered through that East L.A. theater lobby like an enthusiastic Frankenstein's monster, black glasses askew, jeans jacket crunched up under his arms. He was the big success story of the indie crowd, having just come back from Sundance with the promise of funding for his feature. Of course, all the funding later fell through, but that was then. Shirt hanging out, cuffs unbuttoned and flapping, he paused regally before various black-clothed figures to interrogate them about their lives and work. Then he got to me. I told him I was making a documentary about ballet students, and when he said it was a wonderful idea, the roof of the theater seemed to lift off like a hatch, and the blue-black night luminescent with stars made an exhilarated sheen above us. Like I said, that was then, this was now.

In the now lay the litter of Denny's desk, a page twirled into the typewriter platen, about twenty stubby pencils on their sides, and a torn-up sheet with scribbles on it, the daily tally of Denny's nagging obsessive thoughts, the ones that bothered and interrupted him while he was trying to work on his script. Stuff like trash, contacts, UCLA was penciled on the page alongside Sundance, and rent money, the last of which was written about twenty times in all directions on the paper, as if he couldn't believe his magic ritual for banishing bad thoughts had failed him. I looked past Denny, out the sliding glass doors to our parched back lawn and to the lawn chaise our landlord had set up permanently on the slab of cement behind his bungalow next door. He lay out there every afternoon in his shorts. If I happened to pass him, he'd stretch and call out to me, "Ah, California," in the accent of some kind or another, as if the city were still the unspoiled town of blue sky and a thousand orange blossoms.

By the time I made it over to Mona's, it was five o'clock. Mona was in the backyard of her Santa Monica cottage in one of her three-hundred-pound muumuus, watering the lawn. Have I mentioned it was 103 degrees and Los Angeles was stomped flat by a Santa Ana? The grass was brown, unalterably brown, but I watched for a moment as Mona turned the trickling hose this way and that. Then we went inside and she poured us some gargantuan rum and Cokes. Her little boy, Ricky, trailed in our wake with math papers and exercise books. We went into the living room, which was an airy room with a big U-shaped sectional she'd bought somewhere, at some garage sale, with some money she'd gotten editing some documentary, and I put my reels on the coffee table projector. Ricky, who was used to this, settled into his chair with his homework, which we would all ignore.

This was Mona's first look at my uncut footage of the girls in the dressing room, and I was nervous. I turned on the machine, and it threw a square of light onto the wall and then the image of a thin, blond girl with her hair in a bun, sitting on the floor kneading her pointe shoes with her hands. She looked like me at age twelve. In fact, all three of the girls in the dressing room looked like me. They were getting ready for class, pulling on warmers, spraying Hair Net, drinking Tab, concentrating. Not only did they look like me but they were living my old life, exactly, of ten years ago. Or even of ten months ago.

The wall went black, and then up came the girls again, damp and exhausted in that postclass state of ennui and self-assessment.

Girl 1: I saw Margot Fonteyn on TV last night. You know, her feet really aren't that good.

That was true. Mona chortled and lit a cigarette.

Girl 2: In flamenco class you know who's the best one? Athena! And she's short and fat! Too bad for her flamenco doesn't count.

To which Mona said, "Why doesn't flamenco count?"

"It just doesn't," I told her. Not unless you intended to spend your whole career playing the Spanish dancer in *The Nutcracker*.

Mona stared at me and blew a smoke ring.

Girl 3: I've got a major blister on my second toe. It's killing me. I taped all my toes before class, but the tape peeled back during chaînés, and even though I squirted on New-Skin and used two Band-Aids, I could barely stand to finish pointe. I wish I were a modern dancer and could do everything in bare feet.

Girl 2: But who wants to do modern?

"Guess that's like flamenco," Mona said. I nodded.

Girl 1: I ate two bowls of granola, three pieces of toast, and half a bag of Oreos when I got home after class yesterday. I'm going to have to throw up or use an enema before weigh-in tomorrow.

"What?" Mona said, incredulously. She shifted beneath her tent dress.

"She's going to lose her scholarship if she doesn't drop five pounds," I said. "I used to use Ex-Lax."

One of the girls opened up her big leather satchel, too grown-up now to carry the stiff plastic boxes my niece Katie and her contemporaries sported, with the little snap compartments for shoes and the de rigueur pictures of pink-tulled ballerinas. Out of the satchel came leotards, tights, shoes, shoes, shoes—pointe shoes, ballet slippers, flamenco heels—adhesive tape, balls of lamb's wool, Fabulon.

"My God," Mona said. "It's like Mary Poppins's bag."

Girl 2: I had the worst class. I couldn't do *anything*. Did you see me wobble in that arabesque penché in adagio? And I hate Betsey in my car pool. When I cry after a bad class, she and her mother look at each other.

Somebody or other was always crying in the dressing room. Last year it had been me.

Ricky got up from the sofa and began to dance, a none too original parody of a ballerina, the bourrée turn with his arms above his head and a pinched-nose expression.

Up on the wall behind Ricky another girl was talking.

Girl 1: I'm gonna do my eyelashes really long for *Nutcracker*, like fake eyelashes and lots of eyeliner and eye shadow and lipstick. You know, we're like models except better, because models can't do anything.

I turned off the projector and looked at Mona. "So what do you think so far?"

Mona puffed on her cigarette a moment. "I think," she said, "that is the weirdest collection of little freaks I have ever seen."

I said uncertainly, "You really think so?"

"It's totally obvious," she said, and I took a big draw on my rum and Coke.

"Huh." I hadn't even shown Mona the part I'd filmed of the mothers, the ballet mothers, sitting like hawks in the reception area, watching the girls' class through the open door. They knew as much about everything as the girls themselves, who was the most talented, who was going for a summer scholarship to New York, who would probably get to play Clara in the December *Nutcracker*. It took three to make a dancer—a teacher, the girl, and her mother. Behind every ballerina stood one of those mothers, pushing.

Ricky was jumping from the sofa to the front window.

"You know," Mona said. "This whole film is about the way the dance perverts these girls with its unreasonable demands and turns them into competitive backstabbing little mutants."

"But didn't you see how perfect they were, like tiny little disciples?"

"No," Mona said. She stubbed out her cigarette. "Now what we need to do with your footage is to intercut it with some clips of, say, Siamese twins and circus performers, and maybe we can get some film of some real sideshow freaks, like this frog boy I once saw in Tennessee."

She went on, but I stopped listening. Ricky was throwing his math papers in the air and skating beneath them. Okay, so maybe my film wasn't about beautiful little dancers in the making. Maybe I was too recent an exile from the world of ballet and therefore still subject to its unreasonable and blinding power. Maybe the kingdom of the dance was a weird kingdom, populated by mutants rather than disciples. What did I know? I was out here in Los Angeles. I was a freak myself. What did I know about anything?

≈

The Brahmins

When I got home, the house was quiet—Denny was in his hole, the bedroom at the back of the house—and the living room up front was dark and purplish, the color of all evenings in Los Angeles. I sat down in a chair, reels in my hands. Our landlord had left us a few odd pieces of furniture, most notably two high-backed vinyl armchairs that swiveled and rolled on coasters, and a long coffee table that opened up, absurdly enough, into a padded couch that resembled a church pew, and these things looked vague and tremulous in the strange light. It was the time of day when I used to go to the theater to get ready for an evening performance, and it was this time of day when I most often found myself wishing I had never quit dancing, when I missed my sister and little Katie and Jack, especially Jack. In her last letter Alison had written that Jack had a role in the touring company of *Fosse*. He wasn't even in New York right now. He was in Detroit, and if I called him at his hotel, he wouldn't even answer the phone, that's how much he hated me.

From the back I could hear a sudden splatter of typewriter keys. Denny typed with the speed of a thousand executive secretaries. I got up and went into the kitchen. Outside, the flat concrete drive looked like putty-colored matte, and I cranked the slatted side windows closed against it. I put on the light and opened the refrigerator.

I took my plate into the little laundry room off the kitchen that we'd turned into a breakfast nook of sorts—a red folding card table faced the cylindrical water heater and the side door. I crouched down in my very little chair and watched the sky turn to hazy black as I ate crackers and scrambled eggs, the water heater giving an occasional hiss and belch. And then Denny was behind me, the glare of the kitchen light throwing a big monster shadow of him onto the water heater.

"Are there any more eggs?" he said.

"Look in the pan."

He looked and then brought his own paper plate to the table. He'd gotten dressed in a floppy flannel shirt, and he was clutching a couple of papers. While he shoveled his eggs to his mouth with one hand, hunched over his plate, sticking his fingertips into his food, he used the other hand to organize and smooth the manuscript pages, like some ambidextrous insect.

"Katie, I started putting a love story into my script, a love story about you and me. I thought my main character should have a girlfriend, and everything that came out was all about you. I made you into a girl at UCLA." He shoved the papers across the table for me to read. It was a scene about watching this pretty girl with a headband as she bent over her book. Denny had the female character lift her head, and his description of her features was so acute as to give me a momentary shock.

"This is really good," I said.

"Do you really think so?"

"Yeah." I gave the papers back to him. "You should write more about this and less about your mother and your father."

He took a cracker off my plate. "Do you really think so? Because, you know, after you left today I went back to my room and it was sort of dark and I sat down at my typewriter and this came out."

The room felt very hot and close, and I leaned over and opened the back door to the immediate sounds of dishes clinking, hoses watering lawns. Behind my right shoulder I could see the white letters up on the hill begin to glow in the fluorescent night. Somewhere, a phone began to ring. Denny cleared his throat.

"Ka-tie, I don't think I'm going to have the rent money for tomorrow. I sort of balanced my checkbook after you left."

"You went back there after our fight and balanced your checkbook?"

"Well, I'd been thinking about calling a taxi, and I wanted to see if I had the money."

"Was this before or after you started writing our love story?"

"No. I mean, I called the taxi, but then I canceled it. Before I did my checkbook. Before the love story. Katie, it was one of those moments when I didn't know what I was going to do, but I really, honestly, want to stay with you."

"So, how much money do you have?"

"Not too much," he said. "About seventy-five dollars."

"In the world?"

He nodded. He got down off his chair and sidled over on his knees, put his head in my lap. The great indie artist with the cool black glasses and the Frankenstein's monster boots and the Brahmin-size ambition and the Untouchable-size bank account. He spoke. "So do you think you can cover me?"

Both Denny and Mona were with me when I finally made it to the Center for the Dance to film my girls in Studio 1. We had two cameras and all the cables wired up and a couple of sets of lights arranged, and Mona, Denny, and I stumbled around amidst my crew of two while the girls stretched at the barre and waited for class to start. It had been easy enough to get permission to film: half the girls had agents and were carted around by their mothers to various commercial auditions seven days a week. This was, after all, Los Angeles. Then Madame came in and the girls snapped to attention. Denny plugged in the lights, and we were all bathed in a hot, white sensation. We were just going to film the class, there wasn't much for me to direct or do, but still I wished

I'd paid more attention to the way Baryshnikov had rehearsed us in New York. Of course, if I had, I wouldn't have been here. Mona was sweating and Denny was chewing on something, probably a wad of paper, maybe even a page from my notebook. He gave me a thumbs-up. I went behind the cameras and signaled my crew.

The girls began their barre. In first position, their heels together, toes flipped out, they began pliés, moving their arms from the sides down the fronts of their bodies and then up again. The studio smelled like any studio anywhere, of resin and sweat and adrenaline. Just walking into the room had given me a charge. Walking into a studio had always given me a charge, right up until the last day I had done it back in New York to tell Baryshnikov I wanted to take a leave of absence. I squinted behind the camera. The girls looked good, fragile and serious, especially my favorite little blond one, with the white chiffon bow in her hair, as if she were studying dance in Soviet Russia. She was the class star, but the other girls were still giving her a good run for her money. By this age, only the serious girls were still at it. The pudgy and the graceless had dropped by the wayside; the initial excitement of pointe shoes, the carrot that kept little girls tied to the barre, had by now given way to the agonizing reality of them, and a great corps of girls had vanished like shades. By age twelve any girl left at the barre wanted to be Margot Fonteyn and believed she could be. Quit at this age, or at fourteen or fifteen or sixteen, and you'd be haunted by dancing the rest of your life.

Pliés were followed by tendus and ronds de jambe and développés and battements, the whole routine I knew so well, and as I watched them, my muscles made involuntary contractions, something like sympathy pangs. Or jealousy. The class was an hour and a half long, and I filmed the girls at the barre and then at the center for their slow and fast combinations, their turns and jumps. It wasn't until the girls were doing their révérences, the delicate and sweeping curtsies they would eventually do for an audience at the end of a three-act ballet, that I noticed Denny and Mona were no longer in the studio but had wandered off down the hall to the doorway of another room, Studio 3, where they stood with their noses pressed to the glass window. I clumped down the hall toward them.

"What's going on?"

They turned and then parted so I could stand between them. Inside Studio 3 was the Russian defector and ex–Bolshoi Ballet star Alexander Godunov taking class with a motley assortment of adults—some housewives, a few show dancers, and the ubiquitous whippet-thin forty-year-old freak who, like Zelda Fitzgerald, thought she could take up ballet at this age and actually make a go of it. Godunov stood among them, but he was in a class all his own. He might now be living in Los Angeles, he might now be making B movies, but he was still a star-studded Brahmin, a golden musculoskeletal god. He moved with the definition and the attack of one used to commanding the stage and commanding an audience. His hair was blond and long, and his face was fierce, the body beneath it equally ferocious. Godunov had been a guest artist at ABT before Baryshnikov let him go, and I had stood at the back of many a stage he had commanded. And here we were.

I turned away from the door to where Denny and Mona were conferring, and they turned to me.

"This is who you should be filming," Denny said. "You've got this great ballet star right here. This is who people want to see. Nobody wants to look at a bunch of little girls."

Denny had never seen a ballet in his life. The only reason he knew who Godunov was at all was because of the movies he'd made, *Witness* and *Die Hard* and *Waxworks II.*

Mona said, "We could do a feature film. We could get a script together for him and Patrick Swayze about two big ballet stars competing against each other in a big company."

The hall lights put two sheets of glare on the lenses of Denny's glasses, which flickered and sighed as Denny moved, pushing a piece of paper at me. On it, he had scribbled out an example of a scene from the new ballet blockbuster, and Mona looked at me eagerly. I trusted Denny and Mona. They were my only friends out here. It was hard to remember another time when I had other friends. Coming to Los Angeles was like falling off the end of the world: you forgot your old life, it was blinded out of you, there was only the smog, the heat, and your scrambled ambitions. So I looked at the paper. Above the horizon of it my little girls were filing out of Studio 1. Class was over.

It was a couple of weeks later that Denny and I opened up the sliding glass bedroom doors one early evening and sat on the back step drinking Gatorade from the jug. We watched a humming-bird lurch past us into a syrupy bird-of-paradise bush. The garage our landlord wouldn't let us use made a peaked shadow on the lawn. I peered in the purplish light at Denny's typewritten pages, which were thick with dialogue for the feature film he thought I should be making, the one with Godunov and Swayze battling it out on the stage of the Metropolitan Opera House. This scene was set onstage during *Giselle,* and Denny wanted me to demonstrate some of the moves Albrecht would be doing while being forced to dance to his death in the nth scene of the ballet.

I got up and stood on the one good thing about our rental unit: the backyard, an absolutely unadorned rectangle of grass. And on this little stage like a flat patch of graveyard I danced one of Albrecht's desperate variations. He just wanted to stay alive until dawn, but the Wilis commanded him to keep moving, and the variation faltered between various pyrotechnics and staggers. I felt exhilarated to be dancing again. The air felt wet and cool against my warm body. It surprised me that I remembered so much of a variation I had never myself danced but merely watched from the back or side of the stage in my line of Wilis. I pitched myself about the yard, legs like scissors, arms like branches. Denny watched me from the back stoop, and when I finished, throwing myself down on my side on the grass, he said, "Wow."

I stood up.

"You're really good," he said. And he stared at me.

He was right. I was really good. I was a good dancer from a major ballet company, one of the best companies in the world.

"So what did you do in the ballet while the guy was doing all that?"

"Well, I stood back here," I said, "with the other Wilis. And I watched." I took up a position at the back edge of the lawn, near the garage, and I stood on one foot with the other one tucked behind me, arms crossed. "And then, near the end of his dance, I did this," and I stepped onto the other foot.

"That's it?" Denny said.

"Well, sometimes we turned and showed him our backs."

Denny stared at me a minute. "Huh."

And I stared back.

131

Mona, as promised, had collected all kinds of footage of freaks, and we spent the afternoon in her garage cum editing room. To let me into the garage, she'd had to pull a cord that swung the big door upward, exposing the entire room like a stage set. The light in the place was both bald and dim, and I sat down on a typing chair that was swaddled in a sheet, Mona's idea of a slipcover. The editing machine itself was mounted on what looked like a discarded microwave cart. Everything in the garage seemed discarded or bent toward some purpose it wasn't meant for. The microwave cart was a desk, the bookshelf was a linen closet, spewing Mexican blankets and raggedy towels. The bureau was stuffed with papers and reels and cassettes; some of the top drawers were too full to be shut. The portable heater sat on a chair, which was covered with a matching sheet, as was the floor, and all this whiteness glowed when the heater kicked on.

It was winter, or as winter as it gets in Los Angeles, with some crispy sixty-degree air noodling in under the garage door and edging around my feet. I had a headache from it and from what Mona was doing to my film. I hated seeing my little girls in their black leotards and pink tights juxtaposed with contortionists and snake handlers. Mona seemed to me like some huge freak herself as she cranked the film through the editing bay. I let her do it. After all, she was the one who had gone to film school. And anyway, I still had a copy of my original footage on a cassette at home. I'd filmed some more of the girls as talking heads, a few of my favorites doing some improvised monologues about their dreams for the future, but I hadn't shown Mona this yet. She was still at work when I left.

At home, Denny was waiting to show me the latest incarnation of his screenplay, and I had to sit down immediately on our pewlike couch while he watched me read it. I shifted the wad of his manuscript on my knees. Denny's scripts were always incredibly gnarly, that was the one constant, and it took me a while to realize I was reading a lot about a new character, this sluttish Untouchable-type corps de ballet dancer who was trying to have an affair with the Patrick Swayze–type ballet star in order to advance her pathetic career. Denny had her doing things out of some bad ballet novel, like putting ground glass into the slippers of the star ballerina and then stalking the Patrick Swayze character in his dressing room. Her name was Kathy, and when Denny described her dancing her Wili role in *Giselle,* he made her into this big klutz who thought she was standing on her right foot when she was really standing on her left. After a few pages, I socked the screenplay onto the ground, and the pages fell like white lead onto the carpet.

Denny said, "Ka-tie," and he ran around skimming up pages. "What'd you do that for?"

"Burn it," I said.

"Katie, what are you talking about?" He pressed the disheveled pages protectively to his chest.

I said, "If you don't, I will." And I ran into the kitchen to get something, I don't know what—we didn't have a matchbook that I knew about—and while I was bumbling around, trying to get one of Denny's stubby pencils to flame up over the electric stove, he came in, sans manuscript. "Katie, you're going nuts."

"I'm nuts to pay the rent while you sit home turning me into a pathetic freak in your film."

"It's our film," he said.

"That's not my film!" I dropped the pencil, which was incombustible but not unheatable. "Look," I said. "I don't think this relationship is working. I think you should move out."

"You're kicking me out?" Denny said. "I can't believe you're kicking me out."

"Well, I'm the one paying the rent."

"I can't believe this. I'm the best writer of your film and you're kicking me out. I'm the only one who can make a success of your movie. Everybody at UCLA thought I was the best writer at the school."

"You still have to move out."

"I can't believe you're kicking me out. I don't have enough money," he said. "Can you charge a cab?"

And I thought, I'm going to have to call 911 to get him out of here. But instead of calling, I went into the bedroom and pulled out a suitcase, and when I'd filled it with clothes, I dragged it back through the living room and out the front door to the car, with Denny sputtering and flapping at me. When I started back in, he followed me. Evicting Denny was actually easy to do—his possessions had remained, for the most part, in a wall of fully assembled boxes, sides taped and insides loaded. It was all the detritus Denny had lugged around Los Angeles and now would continue to lug. I started dragging one of his boxes toward the door, Denny going, "Be careful, those are all the notes for my script!" Somehow we ended up making synchronized forays back and forth from the house to my car, loading up my trunk, but trying to do it quietly, so our landlord's wife, who snoozed on a recliner chair in her front window, wouldn't wake up to see what we were attempting to do under cover of night.

When the car was filled, we got in and I let it coast backward into the street. A power line buzzed above us, and suddenly the air was fragrant, the way it must have been forty years ago, before Standard Oil and Firestone Tire ripped up the trolley lines, when orange blossoms and lemon trees, magnolia and jacaranda trees, not exhaust fumes, dominated this city. "Do you smell that?" I said.

"I can't smell anything," Denny said. "My sinuses are backed up with panic."

I sent the car tooling and snorting around the flats, heading up La Brea to Santa Monica and then west across boys' town, where kids with open shirts and wild, beautiful faces skulked and kidded while waiting for their johns, and all the buildings were low and crappy—minimarts and storefronts and narrow theaters, legitimate start-up ones and otherwise, trashy bookstores. There was a bunch of boys kicking around the outside metal tables of a Taco Bell, and I wanted to call to one of them to get in the car and have a wild romance with me, two lowly Untouchables in the dregs of the city.

Meanwhile, Denny was whining, "Where are you taking me?" but I couldn't answer him because I had no idea. We fought and bickered our way around the freeways toward Santa Monica, but it wasn't until we went over the final lap of the 10 and through the tunnel into the optical illusion that we were driving straight into the ocean that I got it into my head to dump my passenger at Mona's. What else was I going to do with him? Take him to the L.A. Mission? He could probably set up a cot in her garage. I was so relieved to have figured this all out that I sped along the numbered streets to her cottage and parked in her drive. "Go on," I said. "Get out and ring her bell." The best writer of my film and the best writer at UCLA slumped, forlorn and furious, in the front seat of my car. I reached across him and unlocked his door. Then I got out myself. I could just make out the

135

shape of the garage. Denny hoisted himself out of the car and
went up the steps to ring the bell. On impulse, I ran around the
back of the house. Through the lit kitchen window I could see the
big shadow of Mona, la maîtresse de la maison, as she moved in a
supervisory way through the rooms. Ricky flicked by. The garage
was ten yards from the house, and I ran them, fast, and pulled on
the cord to lift the door a few feet. The electric heater went on,
and in the orange, superheated light I made my way to the editing machine and grabbed my reels, a piece of film hanging from
one like a sad ribbon on a toe shoe. I made it back to the car
before Mona even got to the front door. Not bad for an Untouchable.

Mona ended up with a job editing a game show for one of the net-
works, and I heard through her that Denny was still trying to
pitch his blockbuster ballet movie to various producers and in-
vestors. As for me, I'd taken to lying out for hours in the backyard
on my landlord's lawn chaise, and I'd almost completely stopped
working on my film. Alison's phone calls had begun to sound
worried. One night I watched the cassette of my ballet girls over
and over on my little black-and-white TV. My favorite footage
was the stuff Mona and Denny had never seen, the talking heads,
where I'd stood the three girls from the dressing room one by one
against a blank wall and asked them each a question before the
camera rolled. Where do you see yourself ten years from now, I'd
asked, and, without exception, each one saw herself as Giselle or
the Swan Queen or Nikiya or the Sugar Plum Fairy, center stage.
In other words, a Brahmin. Not one of them pictured herself in
the corps de ballet, a Wili, a swan, or a shade. After all, who
dreamed of standing at the back of the stage, behind the stars, an

Untouchable in a long white line of other Untouchables? And yet, the footage of these girls in class, so intent, so dedicated, so beautiful, told me a truth: they were already Brahmins and always would be. My favorite blond girl with cheekbones like the Urals and narrow, slanting eyes all her own had used her time to declaim, "A ballet studio is the same anywhere: a mirror, a barre, and pliés. And every single dancer—even Pavlova and Nijinsky and Nureyev and Fonteyn—stood in a studio just like mine and did pliés every day. Just like me." To study the art, to enter the temple, was already to be a Brahmin, and the art—I came to understand—needed us all, corps members, soloists, and stars.

So that's how it came about that I put down my camera and ended up using the rest of Alison's money for ballet classes at the Center. I was trying to get back into shape, preface to trying to get back into ABT. I'd been off for eleven months, which was a disaster but, I hoped, not an irreversible one. I was at the barre each day by 10:00 A.M., standing with the housewives, the show dancers, the freak, and the great Godunov. He was a foot and a half taller than I was, with thighs as thick as my trunk, and when he turned from left to right to repeat each exercise, his eyes flicked right past me. To him, I was just another housewife. Who else would be out here dancing, except hopeless dreamers or little girls, who crouched outside our studio doors when their class was over to get a glimpse of the real thing? Godunov, that is, not me. So anyway, there I was slaving away by him in my leotard and tights, feeling a bit like I had back at ABT when I took class with Sylvie Guillem, which is to say, maybe not entirely and fully Brahmin-like, but I was trying not to think about that. So maybe I wasn't of the highest possible Brahmin caste. So what? This was better than watching from behind the camera. And it was certainly better than working at Clifton's. At least at the Met there was a real paycheck and the fringe benefit of reflected glory. There was applause, when I took a bow with my forty sisters. I got to wear fake eyelashes and pretty costumes and to gaze at the likes of Baryshnikov and Godunov and Nureyev and Fonteyn at a range of two meters. And I got to dance. Okay, not with the big Brahmins. At the back of the stage. But hey, one could always look forward to reincarnation.

A Short Season

West Hollywood, California, 1995

He was drunk by the time he got back from the party. He had stumbled through it feeling both hideous and superior, meandering restlessly among the celebrities, ordering drink after drink from the free bar. He'd had a glass in his hand when he saw her, standing with George Hamilton on the patio. He hadn't seen her in three years, and her face caused him the shock it always caused him when he saw it after an absence, though whether it was because it was the face he loved or because it was the face of a movie star he was never sure. He did not approach her: she would smell how much he had been drinking, his tongue, his teeth, his gums soaked in alcohol. So now he was home, where it was dark, and he sat heavily on the leather sofa. The streetlights of West Hollywood cut his body in two. His hair was blond and long; he was so tall his legs were thrust beneath the coffee table he'd bought in New York fourteen years ago, when he still danced with ABT. But this was Los Angeles. It was supposed to be far away and full of lotus blossoms you could scoop off the street and stuff in your mouth any time a moment surfaced you wished to forget. He was

Alexander Godunov, once a young star of the Bolshoi Ballet, briefly an American dancing comet, temporarily an American movie actor, and now forty-five years old and nothing at all.

Riga State Ballet School, Latvia, 1965

In the corner of the studio sat a watering can, and Alexander grabbed it, ran in big circles around the worn floor, wetting it down until Kapralis said, "Enough." He stomped on the big clumps of glowing resin in the box and then stood before Kapralis on the center stage mark, a taped X. Kapralis clapped his hands, gently, and the rehearsal pianist began the male variation from the *Sleeping Beauty* adagio, Act III. Alexander was almost sixteen and already developing a reputation as a rebel, wearing American blue jeans and American cowboy boots, his hair long, shirts unbuttoned low. But none of this mattered in the studio, where he worshiped Kapralis and worked for his approval, as they all did, all the fatherless boys. In the studio he was a boy impersonating a prince, the power of a prince as it was revealed through the slicing entrechats, the syrupy slowness of the perfectly balanced pirouette. His feet were bad, still sloppy, almost flapping at times; occasionally his limbs shot out wildly. Kapralis worked quietly, with his hands, with his soft laced shoes, correcting it all; he saw everything, he was the most beloved teacher of the older boys at the school. Alexander, sweating in his white T-shirt, wanted to embrace his teacher, his god, but he saw in the studio door window Baryshnikov's watching face. Kapralis coached him, too. Mikhail Baryshnikov would be going to Leningrad soon, to the big city, to study at the Kirov Ballet's school. Without acknowledging Misha, Alexander turned away.

A Short Season

Bolshoi Theater, Moscow, 1970

He planted himself at the back of the theater to study the great Vladimir Vasiliev in *Swan Lake,* his arms, his entrances, his magnificent leaps. Tomorrow night, in this same ballet, Alexander would make his debut with the Bolshoi. For four years he had danced with a small company, but he did not want to be small potatoes, had not worked so hard at Riga to do that, had not drunk tomato juice and slept on the wood floor praying to become tall just for that. But he had been a small potato for four years, while Misha was a star in Leningrad. So it would be now for him. Tonight he was back of the theater, but tomorrow he would be center stage, in the black tights and the brocaded tunic, Moscow's prince.

Savoy Hotel, Moscow, 1972

Lyudmilla was only a soloist in the Bolshoi, not a principal dancer like he was. The bar was crowded, and he had her at a table against the wall. She was wearing the cocktail dress he had bought her, black market. She looked better in it than in the studio in her pink tights, better in the mink hat, the black heels, the cigarette held between the ring finger and the third, as she talked. He could barely hear her. She was seven years older than he, and she was smart. He was an oaf. He would marry her.

Sverdlov Square, Moscow, 1974

On his motorcycle he took off down Petrovka, away from the square, from the Bolshoi Theater, going 120 kilometers an hour. His leather jacket split open and cracked like bat wings beneath his arms. He could barely see, his hair had grown so long, a fury around him. During rehearsal the word had spread: Baryshnikov had defected in London while the Kirov was on tour. Like Nureyev, like Makarova, another Russian dancer in the West to be celebrated. And free. Here in Moscow, somebody was always watching Alexander; he was too much the hippie. There were anonymous letters about him sent to the theater, there were rumors, he was asked repeatedly to become a member of the Communist Party. Alexander sped away from the old city to the pillars of concrete office buildings and apartments north of the Kremlin. If he looked back, he could see it, the cathedrals with their yellow caps, stooped against the vast modernity, stooped like old men.

Bolshoi Theater, Moscow, Le Corsaire, 1978

The braided cords of the costume chafed his bare chest by the end of the ballet. He was wet, his hair stinging as it slapped his face during his final variation. He was the lion with the long Roman face, the American hair. With the last twisting turn his arms whipped the finish into something Spanish, something Tatar, and then Plisetskaya was out from the wings for the coda, so quick it seemed seconds until he was stretched on the floor at her feet for the final posture, back arched, arm raised, head in its feathered headband thrown back to gaze at her, both of them triumphant. Then the curtain dropped, tremendous, resplendent, red and gold, with its hammers and sickles, stars, wheat, fleurs-de-lis, fringes, and the Cyrillic lettering that spelled out USSR. The ballet was over, but he was still here.

A Short Season

JFK International Airport, New York, 1979

He could see the plane, swollen and gray, from where he paced. On the tarmac below it, photographers, U.S. officials, Party escorts. The translator was telling him, "She's saying no, she's still saying no," and Alexander grabbed the ledge of the window to stare at the grounded plane, cordoned off, isolated on the airfield, as if with his stare he could climb into the bird and find the smoking section, where Lyudmilla sat, her lips framing that contrary *nyet*. In their apartment, the walls pasted with ancient newspaper clippings of his last American tour, the phonograph playing, they had discussed this. She had worried about what would happen to her family. But she was his wife and this was his moment: he had not been allowed out of Russia for five years. She had agreed. So what was she doing now? He stared. Back in Russia, she would be promoted, awarded a medal, a dacha, she would be a heroine for choosing the motherland over her husband. It was a brilliant maneuver. He had to roar.

Metropolitan Opera House, New York, American Ballet Theatre's Swan Lake, 1979

Makarova's tutu was stiff and just an inch or so shorter than the Russian cut he was used to; it threw off his partnering just that much. Already she had become that much Americanized. He grimaced into Natasha's thickly made-up face beneath its crown. She was smaller than Plisetskaya, and the hands had to be just so, here and nowhere else, for finger pirouettes, the arm raised just to this angle, there were a million things to remember. He was sweating, the lights were so bright and the stage so flat. The front was black ink, the wings full of young company dancers come to catch his debut. It felt like a hundred of them there, packed in, some in street clothes. The stage was cleared for his Act II solo, and he ran down to the center mark, long hair flying, taller and leaner than most dancers. So his feet weren't refined, his arms stiff, he had jump, and when he did the wide circle of barrel jetés, he heard the audience out front rouse itself delicately, and he thought, I traveled all this way for that, fuck you.

West Fifty-fourth Street, New York, 1982

He lay on the sofa with his Stolichnaya, his divorce papers, Tchaikovsky on the stereo. The music was so beautiful, so Russian to him, and the sky outside his apartment was so dark. He found himself longing for Riga, for his wife (now his ex-wife), for his mother, for his teachers, for the buildings and streets and studios of memory. He loved his vodka, it was all those things he missed brought inside of him, and he was lonely, he hadn't fucked anybody in months; he'd been afraid, some reticence, the language, the bodies, the manners were all so different. He was listening to *Eugene Onegin, to Olga sing, To sigh and sigh and sigh, as if I'd lost my mind.*

Metropolitan Opera House, American Ballet Theatre Gala, Rodeo, 1982

In chaps, spurs, hats, they squared off for the centerpiece of the de Mille ballet: the competition. Two Russian cowboys from the American West. The white-haired John Kriza and Harold Lang, the last generation to dance these roles, had appeared in their tuxedos, had done a few signature steps, and had bowed to youth; Godunov and Baryshnikov were the third generation of dancers to inherit these roles, and the face of this generation was red, the hammer and sickle. Baryshnikov was a tiny man, further diminished by the western gear, made faintly buffoonish; with his long limbs, his big American smile, the finger on the brim of the cowboy hat, Alexander owned the rodeo, and by extension the stage. When Alexander let Baryshnikov dance, the audience waited with him, for him. At the music's crescendo, Alexander fell to his knees, put his hat into the air, where it spun like a lasso, like an American eagle, spread his arms to the catwalk above the beautiful American stage, and the audience gave him his reward: You are our beloved.

Benedict Canyon, California, 1982

Her voice was low and thick, and in the dark he could see only her luminous dress, white and strapless, the one she had worn backstage to meet him. It was a bold dress. She shut the door to her car. The air around them was riven, crazed, with honeysuckle, sycamore, eucalyptus. They stood on the gravel path before her white stone house. It was not grand, but it had, on him, a humbling effect. She was rich, a famous movie star.

West Fifty-fourth Street, New York, 1982

Alexander stood, holding the phone. His agent at the other end spoke slowly. Baryshnikov would not be needing his services next season. There were not any ballets for him to dance. Into Alexander's silence the agent kept talking—there were not enough parts, there were so many boys, Baryshnikov himself still had to dance, there were many good companies in America, it took a while to find one's place. What other place? Other companies did

Balanchine, modern, pop. This was the one place in America for a prince. Godunov and Baryshnikov made two princes, two princes from Latvia, two sons of Kapralis, two defectors to America, two lovers of movie stars, two too many of everything. Alexander thrust down the phone and spoke to Misha's specter. "You were always afraid of me. Now you toss me away like a potato peel. Shame on you."

Shrine Auditorium, Los Angeles, Godunov and Stars, 1984

It was a cavernous, concrete space and they had sold only a quarter of the house. It would be a hideous matinee, and it had required, like every date, unbelievable machinery to negotiate and set. He propped open the stage door with a box, and the Los Angeles heat immediately immobilized him. He smoked, squinting and cringing in the brightness. Behind him, the ten dancers he'd hired dressed together; he had the private dressing room, with its white ledge, its black mirror, the folding chair, and a manager, who carried around with her spreadsheets, shipping estimates, and payroll documents, which she constantly made him look at and approve. His technique had become spotty; he was too distracted to give the instrument the focus it required. He sucked his cigarette, squatted in his American blue jeans.

Lancaster County, Pennsylvania, Movie Set, 1984

In the bright sun of the Pennsylvania countryside, he felt good. To the left he could see the two-story barn, to the right, the loop of the hill as it tipped upward. He would turn his back to the confusion of the set, block it out as he had blocked out the chaos in the wings of every performance he'd ever danced. He was simply there, an Amish man flytrapped in the late twentieth century. He told himself this was better than the stage because you could do it over and over, getting it right, the moment didn't slide away from you as it did in the theater, and he knew when he got it right, it would appear that way, over and over, on the screen, for as long as anyone could stand to look at it.

Los Angeles, The Tonight Show, 1985

The cult of the self was a pathetic thing, he felt, as he looked out at the studio audience assembled to admire him. The lights were up because he was supposed to embrace this audience, as opposed to the movie audience he could only imagine, or the ballet audience he was supposed to ignore. He was, here, under the golden lights with them, the lover of an American movie star, a movie star himself now, with his black leather jacket, his red leather pants, his gold medallions. The questions were about his defection, his days in Russia, his life with his famous girlfriend, his impressions of Los Angeles. With his terrible English he explored the tendrils of his celebrity. In Moscow he had been celebrated for his prowess as a dancer, which was a difficult and tedious thing to maintain. He knew: he watched the inevitable and progressive decline of that prowess each morning in class at a small and anonymous ballet school in Beverly Hills. But that didn't matter. This was Los Angeles, and here, fame was about whom you kissed, what you wore, how pretty was your face. It was so easy.

The Russian Tea Room, New York, 1988

The four Russians drank. Nureyev, Godunov, Baryshnikov, Panov. The room was red. The tables around them were bare. Theirs alone had layers of cloths and many glasses. Nureyev sat on the banquette, elevated slightly above them. He pointed to Alexander with his fist full of bread and caviar. "Movie star." Alexander forced a laugh and watched Nureyev eat. As if Rudi had never done a movie. He'd been terrible in them. Such a king. King Rudi of the Paris Opéra. Alexander tipped back his head and took a shot of Stolichnaya. Baryshnikov was staring at him when he set his glass down on the table. The two of them had not spoken all night, had not spoken in the six years since Baryshnikov had dismissed him from Ballet Theatre. Alexander growled, stuffed a napkin in his mouth, and shook his head, a coyote tearing flesh. Baryshnikov looked away. It was 2:00 A.M. Alexander let the napkin drop, shoved back his chair. He should have gone to Europe after Baryshnikov let him go, should have joined one of the big state companies like Nureyev, but it had been good with his American girlfriend. It was too late now. They were all old men. Panov was almost bald, his dark, curling hair vaporized by the long wait for his exit visa. He was the only émigré among them, the rest defectors. Panov had lost his position at the Kirov. Month after month, day after day, he had done a barre in his small apartment, with his beautiful wife, the two of them scraping the floors of the place raw. By the time he got his seat on the Aeroflot, he was thirty-six years old. Bad fortune had stolen Panov's chance in the West. Bad blood had stolen his own. Nureyev and Baryshnikov had snuffled up more than their share of the world's spoils, dividing the continents and the big companies between them, the lords of the dance.

Burbank, Movie Set, 1988

He stumbled about the set of the castle, his face ravaged and dark, his hair combed back and greased, his whole visage a parody of madness, and he cracked swords and unsheathed his knife from within his cloak as the cameras filmed, this time doing the close-ups. It was an easy role; it would not be reviewed. He had been good in the first movies because of beginner's luck, but he knew he had no technique, no training, no craft, and soon he would be found out. Better to stumble here, over the top, in his ridiculous getup, where, beyond criticism, he could clutch the torso of a maiden and spit into the camera's eye.

West Hollywood, California, 1988

From Riga his mother had sent him his old photographs, some clippings, the good-luck medallion his Bolshoi coach Alexei Yermolayev had given him eighteen years ago, before his debut in *Swan Lake*. He was drunk. He lay on the floor of his bedroom closet, beneath the row of clothing bags that held his costumes, the finery for *Le Corsaire, Sleeping Beauty, Swan Lake*. He could see Alexei still, with the thick, white hair as long as his own, the wide black glasses he'd pull off in order to better demonstrate, cajole, mime. He was dead now. What was left for him in the Russia he'd left behind? His father was already dead to him; his mother had aged early, becoming a babushka with glasses in her forties; his wife had remarried. He held the photographs in his hands and smelled the polluted gulf, the sweet mestinsh he'd loved to drink after supper, the pews in the synagogue on Peitavas Street he'd visited with Lyudmilla. He'd brought his bride on a single visit to Riga because his mother could not make the fourteen-hour train journey to Moscow. She's Jewish! his mother had said when she saw her. Yes. Yes, he'd shrugged. So? His mother had stared at him. She'd given him his first ballet lessons at the State school on Aspazijas where he'd met Baryshnikov, and they had begun, as boys, their annihilating twenty-five-year competition. He put the medallion around his neck, the photographs on his chest, crossed his arms. He would never be buried in Rainis Cemetery, in the old city, in one of the plots reserved for the great Latvian artists.

Rancho Mirage, California, 1988

He rolled his clothes into his satchel, which stood open, stiff as a doctor's bag, on the bed, the narrow bed like a prison cot, the whole place was a prison! where you had to pose as if meek, as if penitent, as if you had been a terrible boy. He had had enough of detox. He was checking out. Outside stood the stark, brilliant California desert and beyond it Los Angeles, laid on its back, like a woman, arms and legs open, offering you the chance to reinvent yourself. But he did not want to be reinvented.

Doctor's Office, Beverly Hills, 1993

The kidneys, the liver were plush, swollen black velvet on the screen. The probe moved over his abdomen, over the sleek muscles that sheathed it all in a terrible pretense. The doctor was talking: it was almost too late. Alexander moved his arm: No, death would take too long. A white cloth covered his genitals and legs, the powerful legs of a dancer from the Bolshoi Ballet; uncovered lay the beautiful head and arms of a dancer from the Bolshoi Ballet. In one American moment, the ultrasound had shown him his own Russian corpse, which would stink of vodka even as they buried it. Surely, it would be a painless death, an unknowing one, as he had sat unknowing by his father in the stationmaster's room in the Sakhalin depot forty years ago. His father would not be returning with the family to Riga, and Alexander would never see him again. But he did not know this. He was five. He sat on the bench and looked at all the clocks on the wall that told the time in Sakhalin, Irkutsk, Yekaterinburg, Moscow, Leningrad, Riga, the clocks that marked the westward journey away from his father across every city and zone of the USSR.

Sunset Boulevard, West Hollywood, 1994

The store windows were black with wigs, leather, rock and roll attire, and he slid along them in the blinding heat of Los Angeles in October. The pavement flashed white; the car exhaust burned his flesh and clothes. He crouched beneath the lowered sky, lumbering the few blocks from his manager's office to his apartment. His shirt flapped, his greasy hair clung to his forehead. It had been a few days. He stank. He had a roll of hundreds in his pocket. He went into Tower Records and shoveled CD's into his basket: Tchaikovsky, Adam, Stravinsky, Debussy, Glazunov, Mendelssohn, Liszt, Ravel, Delibes, Chopin, Prokofiev, Shostakovich. French, German, Russian—above all Russian. None of them American. He knew all the ballets that went to this music, every goddamn step, all the staging. The vodka had taken away everything, carved away everything else until there was just this white light in the center, very clear: just the dance.

West Hollywood, California, 1995

He lay on the sofa, the leather cold, and tapped the stereo remote: *Sleeping Beauty*. The "Rose Adagio." The precision of the movements, the clockworklike transfer of Aurora's hand from one bachelor's to another's as she held an attitude en pointe. He remembered the studio at the Bolshoi, the clock on the wall, his legs in woolen tights, trying to keep his muscles warm as he watched Plisetskaya. Every day—class, rehearsal, performance. Every class—barre, center, adagio, allegro, turns, jumps, révérence. Every barre—pliés, tendus, ronds de jambe, développés, grands battements. He needed that order, the discipline of class, of ballet, of the Party, of Russia itself. He would return to it. He would return. The plane would approach from the west, soar over the Moscow River, beneath its metal belly St. Anne's church, the Kremlin with its golden spires. The light was northern, thin. It was winter. It was snowing. There was snow everywhere. The plane would land in the square. He had on his boots, his fur hat. He went slowly up the steps of the opera house, marshaling his limbs through the drifts. His arms, his legs, grew wet. His body stirred on the sofa. The chiseled pillars and pediments had become unruly white shapes. A sudden flurry took his sight away, but in that moment before it was gone he saw what was ahead of him.

In the Kingdom
of the Shades

$\mathcal{W}$e're at my dad's summer house on the Delaware River, in Pennsylvania. He's out back, and Chip and I sit in the dining room in our bathing suits playing double solitaire. I'm beating the pants off him. Chip blows periodic smoke rings to amuse me, and I can see the metal flashing in his molars each time he opens his mouth. The bulb above us burns without a shade, and there are shadows everywhere of our movements. The walls that once had paper on them are now stripped, and the glue has browned, punctuated by long, white stripes. The whole place is in a state of abandoned renovation, my mother's project from when she was still married to my dad. I push up on the straps of the suit I've been wearing all day, and finally I just cross my arms to keep it up. The thing's so old and nubbly you can practically see through it. But Chip doesn't bother to look up.

He's concentrating on the game, working his cards until he can't shuffle them anymore. He's got two long columns and then five stacks he can't budge. I wait and watch him, wondering how long it'll take him to realize he doesn't have a chance. I pile all our butts into the ashtray, and when it gets full, I just let them fall all over the table. After a while Chip quits touching his cards and we both sit there. Chip's a big guy. He looks a lot like one of the stagehands at the Met. He gets up and turns off the dining room light so we can study the night out the big window, and I can hear him breathing steadily and deeply. It's dark and the room feels claustrophobic.

Chip clears his throat. "Truman's coming over tomorrow," he says.

I don't say anything.

"Your dad's been seeing a lot of her when he's out here."

"You're kidding," I say. "She's a big fat hick."

"You know something, Sandra"—he pushes away his cards—"never mind."

"What?"

Chip doesn't look up.

"What?" I ask.

He's putting rubber bands around the cards. "It's getting serious."

"So he told you to tell me."

"No, no."

"Huh," I say. I hunch down over my cigarette so he can tell I don't want to hear any more about it. I light one cigarette with another, ignoring Chip, who's looking at me, I know. Finally, I stand up and go into the kitchen. We have some black-and-white photos tacked up on the wall, and I stare at them, with their white scalloped trim that photos no longer have, framing families, adults and children posed together in rural places I don't recognize. My father's family from Pennsylvania. He has a large family, but in ours there is just my father, mother, and me. Then finally my mother had enough of us and she left, taking her money with her. My father has spread the photos all along one wall and part of another, as if he's been trying to resurrect some version of his old life and dwell in it.

❦

Outside my dad sits in a lawn chair, and I crouch down next to him on the grass. He's thinking about something, probably a poem, and I just sit there by him. The pool we never built is marked off by wooden stakes and rope, and I watch the white nylon catch the light from somewhere, maybe the moon.

It's hard to imagine that at this hour back in New York the company is getting on its costumes for Act IV of *La Bayadère,* the paisleys and cymbals of the first acts giving way to classical white tutus, as Solor and Nikiya go from pre-Colonial India to an opium dream of heaven. The corps de ballet girls are bayadères, the temple dancers, in the first acts, but in the last we are something else entirely, Shades, the spirits of girls who died for love. Nikiya was killed by Solor's fiancée, the raja's daughter, who sent her rival a basket of flowers with an asp curled in the bottom of it. When Solor and Nikiya stand at opposite sides of the stage and stretch their long white scarf over the heads of all the Shades, the scarf unfolds their inchoate longing. Nikiya is dead, a ghost, and Solor has traveled to the Kingdom of the Shades to find her and bring her back. But he can't bring her back.

I'm supposed to be one of those Shades kneeling beneath the long scarf. My costume, with my name, Sandra Ellis, inked on the inside of the bodice, hangs empty on the costume rack in the dressing room. I'm on an unmagnificent leave of absence from the company: I took so many pills I got put in the hospital for a week. I wouldn't let anybody from the company come and see me, but I didn't care if Chip came. Chip's my dad's teaching assistant from the university, part of another world that doesn't matter. He could see me in my hospital gown with my name wrapped in plastic around my wrist. I'd wake up afternoons in the ward, and Chip would be there, by the window, the ends of his hair all lit up from the sun. He made me miserable about swallowing all that Valium. Why'd you do this, Sandra? What'd you do this for? He couldn't figure it out. I never did tell him about my affair with Robbie Perez—he wouldn't have been able to understand it— Robbie was married and a big company star, and I was just a sixteen-year-old corps girl.

After a while my father says, "Sandra, I've been meaning to talk with you."

"I know," I say, and I wait for him to tell me about Truman.

But he says instead, "When I was in the hospital the last time, I was forty-two years old. Do you know how many times I've been there?"

I shake my head.

He holds a thumb to his forehead. "I know how seductive that world is. Sometimes I think if I hadn't had you, I wouldn't have come out at all. But I made a lot of visits there. Too many." He looks at me from beneath his fingers. "How many do you plan to make?"

It takes me a minute. "Am I supposed to know that now?" I ask him.

Chip flicks by the window of the kitchen. I'm sure he thinks my dad and I are out here having a big talk about Truman. He gives us another minute or two, and then he comes out and drops into the chair next to me and the two of them start talking about the book they're supposed to be working on this summer, my dad's memoirs. My dad's a big-deal poet. I just sit there quietly and listen to them talk. I love my father's voice. When I was real little my dad would carry me around the apartment on his shoulders while he worked on his lines. He'd be smoking a pipe, thinking out loud, talking to himself, and I'd feel the hum of it all the way into my sternum, riding high and safe above the streets and cars and whatever went on down below. Back then when he'd have a breakdown and go into the hospital, I never knew where he was, never knew how much my mother resented it. He'd just be away and then he'd be back, nothing compromised between us.

I've always been afraid of being like my father. By the time I was ten years old, I knew before my mother when he was going to be sick again. I'd see him stay up late around the house in his bedroom slippers, grading papers slowly at the dining room table. Some mornings he'd wash and dry his pajamas and put them on again, and then sit smoking, vacantly, in his clean clothes. He could smoke a whole pack, sitting there. I figured as long as I kept dancing it couldn't happen to me. For years it worked. I loved to dance. I used to live for class, for rehearsals. The theater and the studio were always the same, measureless and predictable: nothing there but music and motion.

But after Robbie broke off our affair, I found myself chopping through the barre, each exercise endless and repetitious. The night he told me he'd had a letter from his wife saying she was coming back from Paris, I sat up in bed, sheet around my waist. He'd just finished doing me, and what he said shocked me like an unexpectedly bitter odor. I guess I'd thought she wasn't ever coming back. For a while after she left him, nobody would go near Robbie, but I knew what it was like to be in trouble. I had watched my dad go back to Columbia after the mental hospital, have to face everybody. I saw Robbie endure the graffiti on his dressing room door, put on his costume, go out on the stage. I knew what it had to cost him. I'd go stand by him in the wings, and eventually he started talking to me, nervous before his variations. I'd listen to him, even though with all my makeup on and the same costume as forty other girls, I wasn't sure he knew exactly who I was. But he did. He knew my name, and once he leaned over and kissed my palm for good luck. It was the first time since my mother left us that I'd felt like something.

The next evening Chip and I drive out the highway to pick up some kind of dinner. Truman's coming over after work. I sit in the car while Chip runs into the take-out joint. It's still hot, even though it's starting to get dark, and I fan myself with an envelope I find on the floor of the car. The paper flaps. There's no letter inside, but the front is addressed to my father in my mother's handwriting. The thing has an old postmark. She hasn't had anything to do with him in over a year.

Trash blows across the lot, and a wrapper sticks to the windshield. I have to get out and rip it off. The cars all around me hold big women dressed in muumuus or polyester shorts waiting for their men, too, men in undershirts or sweaty tees who come out the door with bags of barbecue pork and beer. It's like a parody of a crowd scene from a nineteenth-century ballet—the villagers roaming the square—but a grotesquerie, compared with what we do onstage in our rustic costumes and carefully sprayed hair. I get back in the car in my sweaty sundress and dirty flip-flops and sit there with my arms crossed until Chip comes back with a couple of Cokes and the bags of barbecue, like I'd eat any of it. His hair is falling down into his face, and he lopes when he walks.

He's wearing a grimy T-shirt and tennis shoes with no socks. The laces are frayed at the tips like a kid's, and he's got mosquito bites on his ankles. Chip holds out a Coke to me and then narrows his eyes when he sees me staring at him. He knows exactly what I'm thinking, which is nothing good, that's for sure.

He gets in the car, but he won't talk to me. He hates it when I act superior. We had a big fight back in the city a few months ago over that. He'd come to see me dance, and when I'd quizzed him about which girl he thought I was up there, he blew up at me, reminded me he was getting his Ph.D. at Columbia, for Christ's sake, he could sure as hell recognize me on the goddamn stage. Then he pulled out his program and circled my pinpoint face in a row of girls just to prove it. I'd wanted to say something to soothe him, but I couldn't think of a thing to say. But I don't feel like soothing him now, so I just slump against the door and, without a word, he starts the ignition.

Chip's a terrible driver. He goes at a creep, and then he gives the old weathered-black Mercedes some gas and we jerk forward. The wind washes through the car, and my hair blows everywhere. I hadn't realized it had gotten so long again. Tentacles of it reach over to Chip at the wheel, and he slaps them away like they're flies. Along the shoulder of the route, abandoned cars pose, hoods up, engineless, driverless, ghosts. They look like dead animals to me, bad things hauled to the side of the road you try not to look at. Our headlights chop into every one.

And then I can't help it, I start thinking about my pills. I have a bottle of Valium hidden under my mattress. When I get back, I can have all the tablets down my throat in a minute and no one will know. I put on the car radio, trying to get some idiot AM station, just something, but I can't get anything and Chip won't lean over to punch the buttons for me. He's like a big rock in the driver's seat. I put on the dome light and pretend to look for something in the glove compartment, then take out a pencil just to take something out. I draw on the palm of my hand with it, but the lead just rolls along my skin without leaving a mark.

My bedroom here is the little sleeping porch in the back, with a metal cot and a primitive shower. It's not the kind of thing you linger in—a metal ring with a curtain strung around it. In the city I have a tub so deep and wide I can spend an hour in there; Chip would come knock on the door to check on me. After I got out of the hospital, he half moved in with my dad and me in our apartment in the city. Some nights Chip would fall asleep on the living room couch, all the papers he was grading for my dad or the books he was reading a thicket on the floor. If I woke up in the middle of the night, sweating and stumbling around the apartment trying to walk it off, he'd be the only one who knew. He'd cajole me back to bed, comb my hair with his own pocket comb to soothe me. I'd bleached my hair winter white, and I remember it was so brittle, little bits would break off as he combed, feather my shoulders and spine.

When I get out I put on one of my dad's old muscle tees and a pair of jeans that still fit me. I thought I'd gain weight when I quit dancing, but I didn't, I got skinnier, because I've just about quit eating, too. I stand in front of the mirror. With my hair wet and darkened, I look like my mother. At the theater, beneath my black *Bayadère* wig, the jeweled headdress perched like a temple on the mountain of hair, it's her beautiful face I see, not my own. My mom had a mink hat she'd wear with jeweled hat pins sticking out of it and a preternaturally gorgeous face. I pick up my comb and start to work its wide teeth through my hair, long, steady strokes, flipping my head from side to side to get at the underneath parts, short bolts of water shooting across the floor as I rake. I can hear my dad moving around his room above mine. Then he goes down the stairs and out to the Mercedes.

I go sit on the stairs to wait for Truman. The entry windows have no curtains; they're just big black squares pocked with insects and fireflies. As I look, the air beyond the glass cracks into white. An electrical storm. Truman's Corvair comes crunching up the gravel and mud, and I hear her shout when the rain hits her. She runs for the kitchen door, and Chip opens it for her. He's been sitting in there, waiting, too. I can see her brush at her dress with a wad of paper towels. The dress is a wild-looking thing, with straps and pieces of cloth that fold one across the other and a neckline that plunges and blows flowers. Chip tries to help her, handing her the big Bounty roll, taking her purse. Together they move around the kitchen making iced coffee, putting buttered pieces of bread together on a plate. Somehow by the weird misfire of my dad's life Truman's ended up here. She gets Chip to carry the glasses of coffee to the table. When my dad comes in the front hall with the beer we forgot, Chip comes out to help him and stands there motionless for a minute, looking at my shape on the landing until he figures out it's me up here. Then he gives me a reproachful look and follows my dad back to the kitchen. Truman turns on the radio for the weather report. Above their voices I can hear the wind and rain slowing.

When I go down, they're finished eating and sit pushed back from the table. Truman jumps up to bring me some coffee. "How are you doing, honey?" she asks me, and she gets up and down, getting my father a napkin, a spoon, some pie, setting a plate out for me so I can have barbecue. I can't touch the stuff, but she stands there until, humbled into it, I sip at my coffee. I watch the big white wash of her bosom. She's a beautician. She's laid a dish towel across her breasts, and she's giving away haircuts. I look at Chip. He's already gotten his, a flattop, and now he looks like he's in the fifth grade.

Truman goes back to my father. The towel is supposed to protect her dress, but I see little flecks of my father's hair sticking to her forearms. Some fall softly on the barbecue spread all over the table and the brown paper bags standing between the chairs. A nauseating smell comes up off the trash in the sink and makes the kitchen feel tight. My father's face is flushed, he hasn't slept with a woman in a long time, and I find my eyes flicking back and forth between the radio, now tuned to a big band station, and the rhythmic sway Truman has going around and around my dad's chair, pulled a foot or two away from the edge of the table. Part of me wants to run over and put my face into her bosomy towel, and the other part of me wants to throw up. But I don't do either. I just drink my cold, bitter coffee. She tells my father to bend forward and works the small scissors at the base of his skull. When he straightens, his pupils drift slowly, unfocused. He looks like something that's been lobotomized, a procedure my mother had once suggested he consider. The music swings. Truman puts her hand on my dad's shoulder and looks at me. "So," she says, "Next?"

"Me?"

And my father says, "Sandra, why don't you? It's so hot. I haven't seen your neck since you were four."

"I need my hair long," I say. "Or have you forgotten I'm a dancer?" It comes out sounding truculent, and I see Chip wince.

But my father and Truman just look at me.

Chip presses his cigarette butt down into a plate and speaks to me for the first time this evening. "Let's clear this thing." He

starts rolling the barbecue wrappers into the newspapers, and, without looking at my father or Truman, I help him stuff it in a bag and take the trash outside to the Dumpster. The air is clear, the skies above us blue-dark with spoon-shaped stars. Looking up you can feel all the space.

Chip says, "Sandra, your father hasn't forgotten one thing about you. You're all he's thinking about."

"Not all," I say.

Chip lifts the lid to the big garbage can, stomps our bag into a small misshapen parcel, and catapults it into the black Dumpster. We stand there a minute listening to the sounds of the garbage shifting in the metal container, and I lean forward from the waist and stick two fingers down my throat. It's a little trick I learned after my mother moved out, a way to calm down. Chip jumps, scrambling around for something to help me with, like I need help, I've gotten this down to an art, and finally he takes off his shirt and wipes at the sides of my face, holding my hair back. I can see his face is scared in the tiny yellow light we have strung up out here, but I can't say anything yet to reassure him. I'm just waiting on the slow narcotic aftereffect of vomiting. Chip's talking to me, but it takes a little while before I can make out what he's saying. My ears are buzzing.

"Sandra, that night I picked you out in your white costume, I never lost sight of you, couldn't stop looking at you no matter where you went, left, right, back, front. I am so fucking in love with you, Sandra, don't you know that?" He puts a hand up to his mouth and shakes his head. "Jesus Christ, I can't shut up. I'm gonna go in and get a new shirt." Before I can say anything, he turns and goes into the house, and after a minute I see the light go on in his room.

Chip had come to see me every day in the hospital, but I don't

think I ever felt grateful. Suddenly I want to tell him that I am, grateful for that and for the little things he brought me, the little happies: a candy bar, my journal from home, a T-shirt to wear over the hospital gown. It was hard to look at someone in the hospital, stripped, in a blue gown. That night last season he came backstage at the Met and jokingly asked me for my autograph, I laughed. Nobody asks corps members for their autographs. But he wasn't really joking. He gave me his pen and made me scribble my name on his program. With his finger he stroked my signature, *Sandra Ellis,* like it was something precious.

I can't stand the idea of seeing my father or Truman again, so I go around the back of the house and crawl through the window of the sleeping porch. I take off my smelly clothes and stand there. It amazes me that I still have the shape of a dancer: the long muscles, strong back, blue-veined feet—it's really a big sham. I hold on to the door of the closet and do some pliés and tendus and ronds de jambe. In my theater trunk at the foot of my bed I've got the one hundred pointe shoes I won't be wearing this season, tailored for me by my maker in England, with my extra-long vamps and my Philips insoles. They're beautiful shoes, untouched in their plastic bags. I couldn't bear leaving them behind in New York. I thought while I was here I might want to look at them. I love the white ballets, being a swan or a Wili, a sylph or a Shade. The costumes are the same, white tulle skirts, sometimes long and sometimes short, and the lighting is always blue-black, as if we were underwater. Plenty of nights I wished I could stay in that netherworld and never come out. The Swan Queen, Nikiya, Giselle, they all wanted out, to be released, to go back to the real world and to their beloveds, but not me. I just wanted to disap-

pear into the ground, like a Wili, or into the air, like a sylph, or into the opiate haze like the one Shade Solor chased in his white-feathered turban. But unlike those other girls, I didn't die, I just passed out on the bathroom floor.

My feet make noise against the rough wood planks, and my legs and arms and back do the work without me even thinking about it. I've been doing this warm-up for ten years, since the day I took my first ballet class, and the routine is comforting. There's a certain power to it. But it's been months since I've taken class, and I'm terribly out of shape. It would be a long haul back. And when I got there, Robbie would be dancing center stage with his wife, Solor recapturing his Nikiya, while I stood behind them in a line of anonymous Shades—scenery. In the dark bed he had shared with her, Robbie gave me access to him and to an appetite I hadn't known I had. The first time he fucked me, I was scared, but Robbie refused to let me be scared, took me with him, his face with his black black hair turned sideways as he roared. He'd helped me move my theater trunk and costumes out of the big room where I dressed communally with all the corps girls into his own dressing room, and he didn't care what anybody said, wanted me with him there behind his door before his performances, not to do anything to, just to have me there. Later he had the stagehands take it all out. I'd stand on the stage then, numb, my tutu stuck on me, looking at the tape marks on the stage floor and waiting for the whole thing to be over. I'd get home from the Met after and put my practice clothes in the washer, just sit on the bed in my robe, looking at all the ornate mahogany furniture my mother bought me before she walked out, leaving us the apartment in the Eldorado like some kind of booby prize. The whole thing felt like being washed toward a funnel and sucked through. And then one of those nights Robbie came to my door. When he left, I said, Goddamn it, I'm gonna kill myself, chewed a bottle of Valium.

When I've gone all the way through grands battements, I put on my nightgown, but I can't get into bed. I stand there, head turned up to the sloped ceiling, and listen to the house settling around me. I'm sweating. Then I get down on my knees and stick my arm under the mattress. When I hear Chip's voice at the door, I yank my arm out and sit back.

"Come in," I say.

He comes in and sits at the edge of the bed. "How are you feeling?"

"Really great," I say, just to get him out of here.

Instead of going, he puts out his hand. After a minute I give him mine, and he holds it tightly. "Sandra, what I said before, just forget it. I had too many beers." We're quiet. Then he bends his neck and kisses the palm of my hand, and when I don't pull it away, he uses his tongue to lick my skin. That sends a bolt of something strong up my arm. I look down at him, bent over my palm. His hair's as blond as mine. He's shaking his head. "Sandra, you know, you and your father, the big poet, the ballerina. My brain's buzzing." He raises his head. "You know what my shitty apartment looks like?"

I take my hand from his and unbutton the front of my nightgown.

He watches me. "I can't. I can't do this, Sandra."

I open the nightgown wider, so he can see my body. I've got no breasts at all, but still I can feel his breath on me where my buttons are undone.

"What do you want me to do?" He's hoarse. When I take his hands and make them lower my straps, his face changes and his expression becomes resolute and he pulls my nightgown the rest

170

of the way down. He's shaking. "Jesus Christ," he says. "I don't know how this is gonna be," and then we're into it. Chip crashes around getting his clothes off, and his body is big and fleshy, huge, he's like a huge, flabby giant, with a big red dick standing out, and I can feel myself drawing back, but when he puts his hands under me I'm so much smaller he can hoist me right up, carry me to the bed. He looks me in the face as he walks with me, his eyes like green glass, a way I've never seen them before, and I want his tongue again, but I can't breathe right. Even before he's doing it to me, I'm starting to lose it, and just as we get the steel cot slamming against the floor and the wall behind it, and I'm making way too much noise, Chip stops and groans, "I can't do this," and pulls out of me. "It's not right, Sandra. Not with you like this."

My hair is all over my face, and, humiliated, I push it around with my wrists, trying to mop up the tears so Chip won't feel them, but he knows what I'm doing, he always knows what I'm doing. He takes my wrists and tries to hold me still, but I knock him away and climb out of bed. I go stand by the window. Chip watches me, getting ready to say something else, so I turn my back. That's how I see my dad and Truman out on the drive. He's helping her into her old car, holding her hand as she wedges herself into the Corvair. She's still got one leg out when she tips her head up for a kiss. My father bows toward her, and Chip comes up behind me with my nightgown, drapes it over my back and shoulders. He holds on to me through the cloth until the Corvair's vanished and I stop wishing I could get into it and drive away with her.

"Your dad's retiring at the end of the year," Chip says quietly at my back. "He's planning to stay out here."

I turn to look at him. "I'm going to be in New York alone?"

"No. Not alone."

"With my mother?"

The instant I say it, I know it's ridiculous.

Chip rubs his hands over his mowed hair. "I'll be there, Sandra," he says finally.

I stare at what I can see of his face. Is this why my father allowed him to move in with us in the city, brought him out here
with us to Pennsylvania? To replace him? Because of course I
won't be living with my mother. The last time I saw her was five
months ago, just after I was released from the hospital. She took
me to lunch at the Four Seasons. By then I was on medical leave
from the company, but we didn't talk about any of that. I was
supposed to be a ballerina, not a mental case. I'd wanted my dad
to bring my mother to the hospital, but he never did. My first
week there I was so pissed off about it, I wouldn't even talk to
him. But then I figured it out. She didn't want to come. At the
time I didn't even think, Fuck her, I just thought about how,
when my dad was in the hospital, I didn't want to go to see him,
either. I was six when I visited my dad for the first time at Belle-
vue, and I couldn't bring myself to look at him until it was time to
leave. Even now it hurts to picture his face, receding behind the
tiny window of his ward.

In the morning Chip is gone, back to the city to get some papers
for my dad. My father sits in his study with the door open for the
breeze, writing on a tablet. He works slowly. I sit on the porch
and watch him while I shoot my hair with a squirt gun to cool off.
My father's hair is as blond as a child's. He stares for a long period, scribbles briefly, stares. I wonder if it's one of the poems

about my mom. He's got a whole stack of them he doesn't pub-
lish. After she bought her way out of their marriage, I'd waited
for him to go into the hospital again, but that didn't happen. He
started writing those poems instead. In photographs of the two of
them when they were young, they look so sleek you'd think nothing could touch them. My squirt gun is out of water, and when I
get up and go to the kitchen, my dad calls out my name.

I go in the study and stand by the chair in front of his desk.

"Sit down," he says, and I do. Now that I'm here, he doesn't
seem to know how to get started. I look at the desktop. It's not a
poem he's working on but a letter. He gets up to retrieve his
vodka bottle from the shelf, and I sneak another look at the
tablet. "Dear Sandra." He's writing a letter to me. My father sits
back down and hands me a shot glass.

"All I've got," he says. *"Na zdorov'e,"* and we sip from our
pygmy-size glasses. He puts his down. Then he reaches into a
drawer, puts my bottle of Valium up on the desk, and looks away.

I stop drinking.

"When I was a boy, Sandra, my mother hung herself. Out in
the barn on the farm my daddy bought to cure her of nerves."

"I know," I say.

And he says, "You want to know who found her?"

And for the first time in a long time, I feel grateful to my dad:
at least he hasn't done that to me. I wait for the next thing he'll
say. But he doesn't talk any more about his mother, just about the
vegetables that kept growing on the farm even after that winter,
though they did nothing to cultivate them, and his surprise at
that. Tomatoes and corn, fall vegetables like squash and pump-
kin. I put my mouth to my vodka and go with her into the barn,
winter fields, the way it looks here in the fall, sometimes on a

173

Labor Day weekend when the season suddenly turns. And then I realize my father isn't really talking about his mother but about mine. My mother abandoned me, too.

I look at my father, he's looking at me, and then he pushes the vial of pills toward me. "These are yours," he says.

The room is hot. His papers raise their white edges just slightly in the wind from the fan. The pen rolls, clicks to a stop. I know what he has written on that tablet. That he is determined to save me. That he picked me up off the bathroom floor, called the ambulance, and then, panicked, put his fingers down my throat in the minutes before the ambulance got there. That he'll do anything to keep me, turn my mattress upside down, procure me a boyfriend, find me a new mother. I can hear Chip bringing the car up the drive, and I put down my shot glass. The pills rise high in the thin vial; the tablet paper lifts, ghostlike, about it, the kingdom my father will make me renounce. He knows all about that kingdom and renunciation. It is our kingdom, after all, and he will not leave it empty-handed.

White Swan,

Black Swan

He saw the shape of her first, sitting on the white steps that led up to his brownstone, and he stopped halfway down the block. He could see from there she wore a dress under her coat and her hair was brushed smooth over the collar of it. The closer he got to her, the slower he walked, as if he were slugging through the muck of what had gone on between them before. When she saw his face, she stood, and he knew that she had misunderstood what she saw, that she thought herself unwelcome, that she was going to leave, and he stopped moving, afraid to scare her away.

Robbie's face was as beautiful as Lexa remembered it, the face she had fallen in love with before he had even known her, when she was a nobody and he was so famous. She thought at first he was angry with her, still angry with her, and she stood up, ready to bolt. But then he came down the pavement and lifted her against the brick wall, opening her mouth with his own. It had been so long. She clutched at his thick black coat, the padded shoulders, the wide collar to draw him closer, and let him pull her legs up around him. Beyond them floated the sounds of children playing on the blacktop of the Catholic school next door. It was late afternoon, winter, in New York. She shut her eyes, but Robbie had stopped what he was doing, head bent to tug at her gloves. And then he was rummaging through her pockets and down inside her coat, beneath her sweater, until he found what he was looking for: the long, thin necklace onto which she had strung her wedding band, and she heard him slowly exhale.

He was on top of her when the phone began ringing, and she started beneath his weight. Her hair was so long it was everywhere, over her face and his, down his back, under her, across her beautiful tits. "It's all right," he told her, and he made her come anyway, the phone ringing by their ears, ringing and ringing until finally he reached out and yanked the cord from the wall. She opened her eyes at him then. He put his body over hers, his face to her face, his torso against hers, as if he could cover and protect her and shut it all out. He was still holding the line in his hand when he came and he could not let go of it or her. The bedroom was warm and then it grew cool and eventually she took away the cord from around his fingers.

"Who was it?" she said, and he could see on her face she was afraid it might be his dealer calling.

And he had to sit up then and put his back to her. It wasn't his dealer. He was sure it had been Sandra, but he wasn't going to say it. There were so many things he didn't want to say.

Robbie brought her cold cartons of Chinese food from the refrigerator, and they sat in bed together to eat it, using their fingers, looking at each other, not talking. He looked thinner. He had probably been using.

Flush with love and ambition, they had danced together almost every night last year, booked so tightly with company dates and guest gigs that it seemed to her sometimes they couldn't breathe. The night after their wedding their dressing rooms had been filled with white flowers, and at home the bathroom counter was laid out with the pharmaceuticals they used to get through it all. Their limbs rubbery with the wild artificial exuberance, Robbie would roar across the stage with her. They took amphetamines before curtain, Valium when they got home, and then, strung out, exhausted, but still riled up from performance, she and Robbie had often gotten into it. They would argue, Robbie's face contorting as he put his fist through a door or threw something or threatened to walk. Then he would eat a handful of pills and beg her not to leave him.

One night, after a performance where Robbie had lost his way and forgotten a whole sequence of their pas de deux, she flushed a packet of his cocaine down the toilet. While she was at it, Robbie came raging up behind her and split her lip open on the edge of the counter. The next morning facing the company in class she'd felt incredibly self-conscious, as if she were performing her warm-up in the beam of light dropped from a police helicopter, hanging on to the barre in the glare and racket of it. The other dancers clustered around her at break, looking over her lip and the bruises on her face, and management called them both in for a series of meetings. It was midsummer, and *Vogue* had just featured them in a big spread, she in her jeweled white feathers, Robbie kneeling before her in his black brocade, Odette and her

Prince Siegfried, the image of romantic perfection. They'd been married three months, and they nearly skewered the season, and the company, too, the vertiginous effect of their collapsing marriage knocking down everything with it.

The pointe shoe had a hard box, and she couldn't get it to soften, though she'd slammed it against the dressing room bench a multitude of times and then stomped on the box with her heels. She felt panicky and sick: it was a full run-through of Act II, the first time she and Robbie would dance together again before the company as a whole, and before management. What they saw today would determine the casting for this season and for the spring. Even though ABT was her home and she had danced in its studios and theater for ten years, she knew management was still nervous about her *réentre*. She and Robbie made a volatile compound, and management had let her come back only because together they sold tickets. She stuck the shoe in the doorjamb and crunched it, listened to the layers of starched satin crackling.

In his dressing room, Robbie flexed his legs, shook them out. They were stiff, as were his arms, and he raised them and stood there in the dreary space, making windmills. He couldn't wait to feel Lexa again, to move with her at speed and at rest, to hoist her up into the air and charge across the stage with her, to pull her body to his and allow her limbs to unfold along the length of him. He had danced with a series of other ballerinas while she was away, and he had not liked it.

Her hair was unraveling into a ponytail, the edges of her tutu were tinged with grit, and in the humid air of the studio Robbie's image seemed to quiver. It was the end of a long rehearsal, one where Baryshnikov had had to step in again and again, and each time the corps de ballet had shifted restlessly. Robbie ran across the floor to her now and lifted her again into the long, swooping arabesque they'd stumbled through before. Baryshnikov retreated to the mirror to drink his Pepsi, the expression on his face gradually changing from concern to something like pleasure. She knew it was hard to watch Robbie and not feel pleasure. He was simply a great dancer, the best in the company. And though she was tired, she could feel her lips opening, her eyebrows raising, her cheeks making dramatic hollows. It was all Paris Opéra stuff, tricks of the trade she had learned the past season from Nureyev: the extra tilt to the head at a bravura moment, the flip of the wrist when the leg reaches the zenith of the développé.

She saw Robbie note it, egg her on, keeping pace with her, first thrusting her into the steps with his hands, then easing her back against the pillar of his body. The corps de ballet parted and spiraled away, exposing them; Robbie held his hand out to her, palm up, and brought her toward the adagio's elaborate finish, her body and arms and leg bent backwards around him as he knelt to support her. She had danced this ballet with other partners, but they had been only *porteurs,* assistants to lift or balance her as she moved about the stage. With them, she had never understood how Odette's desire for the prince could overthrow von Rothbart's evil spell. It had been just a convention of the fairy tale, something you had to swallow to get through the ballet.

～℮

He saw out of the corner of his eye that they were making a sensation. Georgina was reared back in her chair, not with her customary elbow on knee, and Terry Orr had stood, arms crossed. Baryshnikov was grinning the amazing boy grin that meant he was pleased, and Robbie turned his attention back to Lexa, keeping his eyes fixed on her now, willing her to respond to him. He had learned over the years how to create a hypnotic web around his partner and how to sustain it, his focused study the example for the audience to follow. Lexa turned in his hands and draped herself against him. What transpired between them was that ephemeral something, the chemistry of something private made into something public that could be marketed. Great stage partnerships were what made these old ballets tick. People stood in line for tickets to watch Nureyev and Fonteyn make love to each other in their beautiful costumes, not simply to witness an arabesque or a tour en l'air. They wanted to see a love story, and this was the big one, *Swan Lake,* four acts of love, regret, death, and absolution.

～ℯ

Outside on Broadway, Robbie stood waiting for her.

～ℯ

She fell asleep after, and he got out of the bed. Quietly, he paced the apartment. He had been afraid to call her, ashamed to call her in Paris, so he'd written her, and he was not sure now how things stood between them. The apartment was still, the surfaces of the kitchen phosphorescent. He opened a drawer, found the bottle of schnapps he'd stashed with the silverware, nicked the paper seal with his teeth. He could rarely fall asleep before 3:00 A.M. after a performance. He'd come home and have a drink or take a pill, and after he'd been with Lexa for a while, he showed her what he did when he was alone. She had been a quick learner, but he was not sure he was happy with what he had taught her.

He'd started using when he was fifteen and a student at the company school, miserable with loneliness. His parents were in San Francisco, and when he'd finish classes at the end of the day he'd sit in his residence hotel until it was time for bed, subject to black moods so strong he'd feel he had to use his fists to punch his way out of them. The talent that would make him a principal dancer with the company by the time he was eighteen was also what isolated him, and he began taking the commuter trains from Grand Central to Connecticut and back just to get away from the sweat and the competition and the depression of the studios. Then he found drugs were as good as trains, and soon enough he no longer had time to leave the city and get back. He was busting his ass on the stage every night, carrying the company by the time he was twenty-four. When Lexa began to worry about how much he used, more about the coke than the Dexedrine, he'd tried to stop but found he'd rage at her when he came back from the theater with his emotions roiling, trying to hold her accountable for something, anything.

He took his bottle back with him to the bedroom and stood there watching her sleep. Without her here he had found this room, this apartment, almost unbearable, and he had had to fill it. He put his bottle down on the bureau, but Lexa didn't stir. He wanted to tell her about Sandra. He had not been discreet. He had been too miserable and too desperate to be discreet. The room was dark, the bed a shadowy quadrangle, and upon it Lexa's body seemed to float. In his dreams he had seen her this way, a swimming ghost, white face, dark hair rippling. He'd call to her, and when she wouldn't come, he'd press himself to the lip of the water, or else, furious, turn away into the mud. It was, he had come to understand, the lake of the swans, the one Odette's mother created with her tears, the one the prince and the Swan Queen drown themselves in at the end of the ballet.

He cracked like a whip, totally on, sailor hat tipped backward and white bell bottoms swinging as he rocketed through the steps. He was dancing *Fancy Free,* a Jerry Robbins ballet, and he had the plum role. In most ballets he found himself strait-jacketed, portraying a prince, but for this ballet he could be rakish, boyish, purely American, with his shock of jet black hair and his face like a goddamn movie star's. The first time he had danced this ballet with Lexa, reeling her around in her high heels, he had shouted, "Ooh, baby, you make me feel so good."

He had noticed her at once when she first took company class, her copper-colored hair and the undisturbed surface of her demeanor suggesting an energy within her that had yet to be awakened. But he was a principal dancer in the company and she was in the corps de ballet, and he was rarely cast with her. After *Fancy Free,* he asked to partner her in something else. Their first rehearsal for *Swan Lake* even he had been surprised by the erotic synergy that erupted between them, which had at first embarrassed him in front of all those répétiteurs and coaches in their chairs at the mirror but then had taken him beyond embarrassment. He had waited for her outside the Met, not caring what she thought of him, that he was an asshole or a star-tripping Lothario, caring only that what she had provoked only she could soothe.

Tonight she was in the audience, and he was aware of that as he moved, aware too of the way his generous charisma touched so many people, both in the house and on the stage. The girl he part-nered tonight was young, not quite seventeen, and he knew he had taken advantage of that, and of her delicacy. She was thinner than Lexa, smaller and smaller-boned, with carefully etched features that were almost shockingly beautiful when she took her hair down, too severe when she did not. He could not look San-dra in the face as he danced with her or tossed her his hat, but he could not avoid the terrible pliancy in her body as he grasped her in his arms and spun her across his back in a cartwheel, stooped beneath her weight. What had happened between them he wanted to keep hidden, but a ballet company was a small place, and the stage was merciless in its exposure.

At the stage door, Lexa stood off to the side and watched Robbie sign autographs, some on programs, some in autograph books, his face drawn, long, dark coat, black beret: *Robbie Perez, Robbie Perez, Robbie Perez.* She had stolen that beret for herself the first winter months they were dating, that and his flannel shirts, his long warmers, even his wool socks. She had been so eager to marry him. They had been in such a hurry to do it the costume designer for the company fashioned her something from an old tutu and headdress on a day's notice. After the ceremony, Robbie had had to reach under layers of tulle to get to her.

The crowd around him was now thinning. Periodically the door would open behind him and a company dancer would emerge, stage makeup still around the eyes. Lexa had bought the American papers in Paris to keep up with everybody, and she saw how *The New York Times* made a big deal about Robbie's stage presence becoming so deeply enriched by his personal troubles, about the gravity he now brought to his classical roles. While he was capitalizing on their publicity, she was sweating bricks every day, struggling to get used to the raked studio and stage, the flamboyant style the Opéra favored, Nureyev's tempestuous rehearsals, where, sometimes, in his frustration, he pushed and shoved at the dancers or pitched objects at them, shoes or plastic cups. She had endured it because she had nowhere else to go and because she thought she was adding to her repertoire, developing her talent. But what good were all these new things if she couldn't use them here? They didn't have raked stages in America, and Americans didn't like ornamental dancing. Even the small following she'd gotten as *la ballerina américaine* counted for nothing here. Dancing in Paris, City of Lights, was like dancing in a black hole—nothing came out. No news traveled, and whatever reputation she'd staked there, stayed there. And now she was here, standing at the stage door of the Met, watching Robbie among his fans.

The stage had been cleared of the scenery for *Fancy Free,* the set that looked just like an Edward Hopper painting with its flatly colored bar, and in its stead had been erected the pillars and tapestries of the palace ballroom for Acts I and III of *Swan Lake.* The ballet would run for the next two weeks, and the entire company had been assembled on the stage for a full dress rehearsal. The houselights were up, and from the wings, Lexa peered out into the rows of red seats. The Paris Opéra was also red, but the house not this cavernous, or this new. The sets for some ballets were a hundred years old, the machinery that moved them massive and antique. The Met was as big as an airplane hangar, and, except for this ballet, the house almost impossible to fill. For Act III the stagehands produced all kinds of crowd-pleasing tricks, puffs of smoke, lightning, the quick projected image of the Swan Queen Odette writhing in despair when von Rothbart's daughter, Odile, impersonates Odette and bewitches the prince into betrothing himself to *her*. Odile was the black swan, and her costume was a short black tutu with a plunging bodice.

Lexa paced in the wings with her warmers on beneath the dark tulle, working her feet in their pointe shoes, trying to keep her muscles ready. Her entrance in this act was a late one. Robbie stood on the stage already in his own black-and-gold costume, the one he'd had custom tailored for eight hundred dollars, while the Queen urged the prince to select a bride from the line of corps girls. Robbie danced first with one princess, her ball gown flaring, and then with another, working his way down the row of them to please his mother. The delicate blond girl downstage left reared back slightly as Robbie approached her, and Lexa watched the way he had to pull at her arm to bring her toward him. She saw how the girl would not look at him at first, and how he would not look at her either, until he had set her back into her place. The girl raised her chin at him then, and Robbie paused for a moment, something twisting across his features before he turned away. In the wings Lexa held onto the black folds of the curtain until her breath had steadied. Robbie's back was to her as he mimed his rejection of those girls to his mother. He had written her in Paris: *Lexa, you're the only white light I see.*

By the time they got back to his brownstone on Tenth Street, Robbie was limping, some pain in his shin bothering him so much he moved down the pavement like an old man. He had landed oddly from a jump, and he was distracted by this as Lexa followed him quietly up the stairs and into the apartment. He grabbed a bag of ice from the freezer and held it to his leg before he noticed exactly how quiet she was being, and when he looked into her face he saw it was the face she wore when they were about to fight. She had worn this face the night he twisted her arm and bent her head into the bathroom sink, splitting her lip, when for a moment he thought he had cracked her head open. The next day she'd had stitches and a thick flag of bruises across her face, and everybody in the company had cut a wide swath around him. He'd gone from star to pariah in one instant.

He watched her sitting on the edge of the straight-backed kitchen chair, her head down, her beautiful coppery hair slipping over the front of her winter coat.

"Are you still seeing her?" Lexa asked him without looking up.

He thought about stalling, denying it, but then shook his head. When he'd told Sandra Lexa was coming back to New York and they would have to stop seeing each other, she had sat up in bed and cried silently, her face streaked with tears and mucus, and he had had to sit there and watch it until she stopped, nothing he could do. He put his head in his hands. "Lexa, I was just so goddamn lonely."

"So you had an affair."

"I didn't know it was an affair," he said. "I didn't know what was going to happen between us. You ran out on me, remember?"

"I didn't run out," she said.

"You couldn't wait to get away from me, and I was stuck here with all this shit—girls refusing to dance with me, management wanting to can my ass."

"It was my ass they canned," she said.

"Bullshit." And he felt the familiar irritation billowing up from somewhere in his gut. He let his breath out and said, "You begged Baryshnikov to make that call to Paris. You wanted to see if you could make it without me. And now, you're back, so I guess not."

"I was promoted before *Swan Lake* with you," she said.

"Yeah, promoted and standing there," he said. "Doing nothing."

"I was doing plenty in Paris."

"You couldn't even have gotten that gig in Paris if it weren't for what we did here. Paris was so great, get back on a plane." He stood up and threw the bag of ice in the direction of the sink. "You want to do our dance, let's do it. But don't lecture me. Don't even think about it. I'm the great fucking Siegfried. Without me, you're just a big flapping bird."

She vaulted toward him then, and he grabbed her by her shoulders and carried her backwards, crushing her into the wall. She screamed and kicked and flailed at him as he lurched with her, but her boots only nicked at his thick coat. She worked her beautiful face and then spat at him, and when he felt the spittle hit his cheek, he drew his fist back. At her shout he sent it slamming into the plaster by her face before dropping her and turning away, pacing—"Fuck, fuck, fuck"—pulling at his own hair. He went from room to room and eventually went into the bathroom and shut the door against the sound of her wailing.

～⁎

A few minutes later she was alone in a cab, weeping and using her gloves to sop up the mess.

~≋

He scrounged up some pill from the bottom of his pants pocket, a Valium, and threw it down his throat while he paced. The apartment was cold, and there was nothing in it but some sticks of furniture and the fight they just had. He was sweating, and he put a hand to the back of his neck. He had promised himself what had happened between them was not going to happen ever again, and Lexa had been back two days and it had already happened. He needed her and he hated that need, which was to hang the heavy rucksack of his sadness around her neck. The Valium had made him queasy, and he squatted a moment and panted, miserable. He could not see her wanting to go on with him now. Even as he had picked her up and carried her to that wall, he had been telling himself to stop, to put her down, let her go.

He couldn't stand to be alone here again.

~≋

He knew where she lived, and he knew, too, she would come to the door when he knocked, and she did. Her hair was down and it was so pale it looked like the hair of an angel, and she reached up her arms to him. He kissed her, and in her mouth and breath he tasted a sweetness he did not want to let go of, and for a minute he worried what she might taste of him. He wanted what was pale and small and golden about her, something he had reached out and sucked at while Lexa was gone; he needed that again. He had kept Sandra by him almost always once he had discovered that she would have him, kept her at his apartment and in his dressing room, as if she were a toy or a doll or a charm that he could treasure and then toss. And now have back.

~✤~

When she got to her hotel, she went first to her suitcase for her weed and rolled herself a quick finger of it. Marijuana *après le théâtre* was a new habit she'd picked up in Paris as an étoile. She sat there on the hotel bed with her coat still on and smoked and stared at her suitcases, which she had not yet unpacked. She shouldn't have come back to New York, no matter what he wrote her, no matter how he swore he was a new man. She should have remained an exile in Paris like Nureyev, with his boots and his coat and his leather cap. But she didn't have Nureyev's talent or his charisma or his fame. She was an ordinary dancer. Solid. Reliable. A workhorse. She'd still be in the corps de ballet if it weren't for Robbie, and without him it wouldn't be long before she'd be back there, first one role, then another withdrawn from her. She pinched out her cigarette in the hotel ashtray. Without Robbie she *was* just a big, flapping bird.

~✤~

He woke before dawn. He touched Sandra's hair, looked at the clock she kept on the mahogany bureau. It was 5:00 A.M. He could hear her father moving at the end of the hall. He sat up, wondering how he was going to get out of here. Lately it seemed he had begun to feel safe only on the stage in the privacy of a costume and a role, where all the girls were princesses in their layers of tulle and their makeup. He loved the glitter of the girls and the painted scenery that looked like color on cloth but at a distance became a dense forest, the great hall of a castle, or an enchanted lake. It was hokey, hokey, he knew, but he loved disappearing into a fairy tale, and when the set was broken down and the

191

dancers packed into the bus or plane for the next city, Robbie felt lost. The chairs and the beds and the bureaus of the various hotel rooms were disorienting and unwelcome interstitial props. He skimmed through those moments until he could be back on stage in the yellow heat, ballerina in his arms, both of them transformed.

He was a shit and he knew it and this girl did not deserve this, but he wanted to be home in case Lexa should call him.

The two costumes hung in her dressing room, white swan, black swan. In the speaker Lexa heard the call for places; the orchestra started the overture. She got up and hobbled over to the dressing table to deal with her lashes. She had time. She wasn't on until Act II, when she slipped out of the moonlit lake and for a few hours turned once again into a woman. After three tries she got the lashes glued down, wet the sponge for the Pan-Cake, watching the edge of the sponge grow orange. She painted her eyebrows into grand arches, brushed glittering powder at her temples, the base of her neck, her shoulders. She anchored the crown with a long series of hairpins. She screwed in her earrings, sprayed her hair until it stiffened with lacquer. She turned left profile, right, full face. Queen of the Swans.

He was twenty-one, and he stood center stage with his birthday gift, a crossbow.

By Act IV she hid in the middle of a fluttering circle of exhausted corps girls, crouched beneath a collar of stiff tutus. Robbie, in a fury of penitence, peeled away at them until he found her, trembling with the wound of his unwitting betrayal, and he knelt, pulled back her winged and rippling arms, first one, then the other, to reveal her face. She stared at him. The lights were hot. It was the moment in the ballet when they understood they could not be together, all was ruined, it was over, von Rothbart had won, to be together they would have to die. The stagehands turned on the fans before the dry ice, and the air grew misty. Then, suddenly decided, they clasped hands and ran up the long ramp, pitched themselves off the cliff into the lake. But they did not die. In one of the mysteries of the ballet, they slip through Death's grasp and are last seen on a small golden boat, sailing across the stage behind a scrim meant to signify a world beyond. It was a transcendent moment from the front, to watch them move from the black water to the white beauty of that scrim and the blaze of stage lights. But for them, the canvas was a glare of white, the lake water a pile of old mats, the boat a shell—open in the back—that ran on an iron track. Their balance was precarious, and they gripped the mast. Their faces were thick with Pan-Cake, their costumes soiled with sweat. The boat moved forward, and they surveyed the golden kingdom of love.

In the Wake

He waited, panting, on the small Princeton stage, his bare chest wet, his hands slippery as he clasped the hands of the other dancers to take their call. They had just performed *Departure,* Joe Alton's masterpiece, and Adam had danced his godfather's old role. Randall had been a noble executioner turned boatman, with a burnished gold helmet and a red swash of cloth draped over his torso like the toga of a Roman senator. And though Adam wore only white tights and a pewter headpiece, he felt Randall's presence beside him under the hot lights. The sensation was so strong he could almost see his shape downstage right, tall and broad-shouldered, the thick thighs whittled into slender calves. It was Randall before he had gotten sick, and he stood there on the stage watching Adam, his hand raised.

The parents of the other student dancers came backstage afterward, bearing flowers. Adam hunkered down alone in the boys' dressing room with his towel and his dance belt and his pile of clutter. He sat holding on to Randall's benediction and to the satiny edge of his own triumph. He had been a lackluster student at the High School of Performing Arts, but Princeton had changed that. The heavy Graham work had transformed his body, and lately he had begun to manifest an intensity and an assurance that made others take note of him. Tonight he had owned the stage, and he had not known before what that was like. He used two hands to smooth the longish blond ponytail he had grown the past year and a half. He was prepared to wait here until the last dancers were gone and it was just the crew sweeping down the stage, shutting off the lights. It was December, and Christmas break started tomorrow. In two hours he would drive home to New York City, to the parents he had not invited to come see him dance.

The loft was just as it always was, the living room area a big empty space his mom used for rehearsals, and Adam stalked it with his bottle of beer. Nailed to the walls were the masks she'd collected on her tours with Martha Graham's company. She was gone now on a solo tour, wouldn't be back until tomorrow, forty-five years old and still at it, for Christ's sake. Lucia Borg, Graham goddess. He dreaded the day she would come to Princeton with her sheaths of fabric and her wire mannequins and her cages and her zithers. As her body declined, she relied more on props, but the loft was empty of them now, and empty too of Christmas decorations. From the big windows he could see the lights strung across the next building, a wreath over a doorway, trees pocked with colored bulbs. Even on the years his mother had decorated, she never did much; they always spent Christmas Day at Randall and Joe's.

Down at the other end of the loft, his father dawdled at the black grand, fingering various compositions and recording them on a monstrous waist-high reel-to-reel tape machine. He did this the way other people watched television, as a form of brainless amusement, sometimes used the music for the stiff choreographic inventions he'd foist on his students. His big hands moved over the keys, the chirps and plinks like grasshoppers set loose in the loft. His dad's hands showed none of the arthritis in his hip that had ended his career, forced him to retire at thirty-eight. Randall used to call his dad King Triton, but he didn't live long enough to see what happened to the king. Or to the queen.

Adam hadn't wanted either of them to see him in *Departure*. His parents had made it occasionally to his high school performances, when dancing had meant nothing to him but the family business, but their arrival backstage in their black clothing had always been irritating. The other students clustered around them as if his parents had been the ones to perform. At first, Adam had enjoyed the celebrity of being the son of two famous dancers. But then there was all the fawning and the girls who wanted him to bring them home. He wasn't prepared to do that, to have the three of them perform for anybody. It wasn't much of a show.

Adam took out another beer, popped the cap into the sink. At the sound of it, his father looked up at him, smiled slightly. Adam saluted him with the bottle. He had been here an hour, and it was the first time his father had looked at him directly.

In his bedroom, his old poster of Hendrix still dominated one red wall, stuck up there with X's of tape, but the surfaces of his bureau and desk had been cleared and his bed stripped. He lay down on it anyway and stared at the ceiling, raised his arm to whip up a current of air. His fleet of model planes vibrated. When Adam was six, Randall had helped him hang his models with fishing wire and then had played them with him. They'd battled the Cessnas and B-52s until the planes swung or churned in a vortex or smashed into one another in an exhilarating midair collision. Five years later, his room had been transformed again, from an airfield to a hospital ward, with a metal-railed bed, a portable toilet, a wheelchair, and a washtub.

When the nurse bathed Randall at the end, she couldn't use a washcloth: his skin had become too sensitive. She would soap her fingers and slide them gently across his body. Adam crouched outside his room and watched it all. When the bath was over, Adam came and sat by Randall's bed to read to him from his big book of fairy tales, holding up the best color illustrations so Randall could see them. His mom was doing her West Coast season with Graham's company and his dad was touring with Joe's; if Randall were well, he'd have been off touring with them and Adam would have been batted back and forth between his parents like a fly, but because Randall was sick and the nurse was there, Adam got to stay home. When Adam finished reading, sometimes Randall would draw if Adam propped up the paper. He'd sketch the fairy tales they'd just read, but he put Adam in them and gave him the swords or the flame to destroy the ogres.

A parade of visitors went through the room each week. Adam saw them all, the dancers from Joe's company, sometimes Joe himself, alone, never with his new boyfriend. Joe had begun an affair with one of his new dancers, a boy named Eric, and he was too busy alternately fucking him and creating new work for him to visit Randall often. When Joe did come, he sat by Randall's bed in his baggy pants, his slick ponytail tied up with what looked like the big rubber band from the Sunday paper. He jawed and gesticulated the whole hour. Once, a man in round-toed tennis shoes came and stayed all afternoon. He was a friend of Randall's from Princeton. After he left, Adam climbed up into Randall's bed, which was strictly forbidden, to hear about him, and Randall told him that man was a famous painter. He had been his roommate at college. Randall described to Adam the grounds of the campus, which unfolded before them like the triptych frontispiece in one of the fairy-tale books, a pastoral heaven of paths and grass and stone buildings where men could make magic with their lives.

When he woke in the morning, it was almost noon, the loft filled with winter light. The walls of his room did not reach the ceiling but stopped at ten feet, and Adam had always felt as if his room were a place he could float right out of. The big canvases Adam had inherited from Randall he had never hung but stacked five thick against the long wall, their backs and wooden supports visible. The paintings were worth hundreds of thousands of dollars. Randall had left his parents money for Adam and for Princeton and for the note on the loft. The rest of the money was for Joe and, after Joe went home to Memphis to die, for the company, until his father and Sam Leavitt ran it into the ground. Randall had collected both art and art books, and he had left the books to Adam, too. After the funeral, Adam had spent weeks looking through them, studying Randall's marginalia, his warped, idiosyncratic handwriting, the observations and exclamations, wanting to see exactly what Randall had seen, to know exactly what he had known. Because of Randall, Adam had meant at Princeton to study art, but he'd been ambushed there by his first dance class, by a variation from Paul Taylor's *Aureole,* one of the most beautiful pieces Adam had ever done. The studio had become his comfort;

he needed the wood floor beneath his feet, the pressure of the air against his legs and arms, and as he had become accomplished, more than accomplished, he had forgotten about looking at paintings. They were so still.

Adam got out of bed and went to his desk, the top of it barren. When he had left at the end of the summer, it had been covered with junk. He'd spent the days sanding and framing wood for his mother's various props while she rehearsed her dances in her footless tights. At night he'd walked the neighborhood, looking at the streets and shops his mother had never, in her twenty years in Lower Manhattan, bothered to explore. He brought back bits of stuff from the junk shops, then glued and nailed them into various constructions—big ones for his mom and miniature ones for his own amusement, a metal topiary, a jeweled robot with intricate outer and inner parts, a thick-thighed pine-cone odalisque. He had piled them on his desk and the floor around it. Where were they all? The room was stripped and sterile, mopped as clean as it had been after Randall's last hemorrhage.

His mother had arrived sometime in the morning while he slept, and she sat at the table by the stove with her cup of coffee. Her black hair stood in the Barbie doll ponytail that had been her trademark in the eighties, when she had been dramatically, spectrally gorgeous, too gorgeous to look at, but now her face was drawn and she was thin, thinner than when he was here this past summer, the muscles of her bare calves and thighs too clearly delineated, like the four-thousand-year-old man found mummified in the mountain snow. Her thin arms and thin hands moved restlessly around her coffee, stirring at it, pushing at the cup as she talked to his dad, who stood and walked from the table to the stove to the table. They hadn't seen each other in some months. Adam stopped in the doorway of his bedroom and watched his parents: they were nervous together.

He was struggling with his tux for Sam Leavitt's Christmas party when his dad stepped into his room, glamorous in his own custom-tailored duds. Everything his dad did—move, dress, dance—he did effortlessly. He had been one of Joe's prized dancers, and when the company collapsed, he was put out to pasture at Juilliard. He almost never talked about his teaching, as if it were an embarrassment, that failure of his body. He would probably rather be making a fool of himself with props somewhere than standing at the head of a classroom. Adam saw something of that same frustration on the faces of his teachers at Princeton, in the way they too fully demonstrated the exercises for the class.

With his dad watching him dress, things went from bad to worse, until finally Adam let go of the end of the cummerbund and his dad said, "Here, let me try." Adam stood sweating inside the white shirt and the suspenders and the bow tie and the stiff black pants. His dad hoisted the cummerbund into place and fastened it.

"How was the semester at Princeton?"

"Good," Adam said.

His dad nodded, held out the jacket. Adam hesitated.

"Dad," he said, "was someone staying in my room while I was gone?"

His dad brought the jacket to Adam's arms before he spoke. "I let a Juilliard student stay here for a few weeks."

"While Mom was gone?"

His dad nodded. Adam put on the coat, buttoned it.

At the party were two generations: his parents' and his own, the dancers, choreographers, and composers of the seventies and eighties, and their students from NYU, Paul Taylor's apprentice company, Juilliard, Joffrey II. Adam stood with the students at their end of the living room, by the seventeen-foot tree that looked as if it had been dropped from the set of *The Nutcracker* or brought in from Randall and Joe's old apartment. Sam's latest girlfriend stood with them. She was a twenty-year-old violinist, one of Sam's students from his master class at Juilliard, and she was asking him, "How come you're not living in the city and going to Juilliard?"

"I've lived in the city all my life," Adam said. "I wanted to get away."

"With your parents here? And all the dance companies?"

"Who are his parents?" a girl in a feathered dress asked, and when Sam's girlfriend said, "Frankie Smith and Lucia Borg," the girl turned to him with interest.

Adam looked past her and the big Christmas tree to the great Frankie Smith and Lucia Borg. His father and Sam and Sam's crony John Cage were over by the couches; his mother stood on the other side of the room with some woman Adam didn't recognize. His dad was gesturing, dramatizing a dance movement. Cage laughed. His mom put out a high-heeled foot, postured. Paul Taylor came over and took her hand, kissed it. She turned and went with him to the bar; tall and round-shouldered, he stooped over her.

Adam drank four martinis and made out with the girl in the

feathers, a speaker full of Christmas music blaring behind them. When they paused for breath, he saw his father had broken away from Sam and Cage and had begun moving toward him. And then he saw that his father was moving not toward him but away from a girl in a white dress who shadowed him and who, when she reached him, pressed one hand to his father's lapel. The back of his tux was wet with sweat. She spoke to him, and he lowered his head. A hank of hair cleft his father's forehead in two. Adam looked around for his mother, to see what she made of this, and he spotted her on the other side of the bar, a few paces away, fumbling with a cigarette, oblivious. When she raised her face to exhale, she had on what Adam thought of as her stage face. She was thinking about some dance, she wasn't even here, and Adam felt the lip of the exasperated rage he'd experienced many times before with her, when he'd stood at her side with some toy, or bit of news, defeated, his desire to have her attention eventually diminished by his repeated inability to command it.

Adam felt the girl behind him pulling at him. He let her pull his face back to hers.

Pieces of feathers from her dress were still stuck in places to her flesh, though he'd peeled the dress off. Her limbs were long; he knew nothing else about her, but he knew she was a dancer. Her place was a narrow railroad flat with the bedroom at the back of it and a mattress on the floor. She pulled him down onto it, and they kissed, separated, kissed again. Her skin tasted of palm oil. He could taste her, but he couldn't see her; instead, he saw his father's face, and he operated before the image in a haze of sweat and rage. He grasped for the rubber, the girl beneath him a blur. He couldn't get his eyes to focus, and he strained at the wall behind their heads, which was marked with bits of tiny graffiti done in various colored pens. The letters seemed to sweat and pulse along with him in the small room. He let out a cry, and then he felt with surprise the girl moving below him. He'd almost forgotten her.

❧

On the train back to his parents', 3:00 A.M., he kept his head down in his hands. The car was empty and it rattled and the overhead lights went off and on. He felt sick as he always did when he made love to a stranger, but there was safety in making love to a stranger. He could smell this girl on his fingers, and he took them away from his face and studied them. He had inherited his father's large hands and, along with them, his father's beautiful face and body. At Princeton, he was constantly propositioned by the girls and even the boys, but he never went with them. It was enough to know how their bodies looked and felt and smelled in the studio; it would have been too much to know any more or to have them know more of him. He had sex when he had to with a body he would never see again, and now this seemed to him wrong and terrible and utterly self-serving. He just wanted to get home and take a shower and fall asleep and ignore Christmas Day, which, he supposed, had already begun.

❧

But his mom was sitting up in her ridiculous butterfly chair, a relic from the fifties that threatened to close up on her like a lily pad. The living space spread itself out around her and lapped at the edges of the walls. She was staring ahead as if she could see something. But there was nothing. Adam shut the door.

"Mom."

She turned to look at him. "Your dad stayed late at the party," she said, and she put out an arm. "Merry Christmas, sweetie."

"Merry Christmas," Adam said, and he walked into the empty room, stood with his back to her to look out the big windows at the blinking lights on the opposite building.

"Last year I was in Paris at Christmastime," his mother said behind him, "and everything was lit—the Tower, the Champs Élysées, Pont Neuf—"

"Mom," Adam said. "What happens with you and Dad when you're gone?"

"What do you mean?"

He turned to look at her. She was struggling to sit up in the curved sling of her chair.

"Do you call each other at all? Is it like you're still married?"

She put out her hand to make him stop talking, but he couldn't stop.

"Maybe you should quit dancing and keep him company."

"I can't," she said, "and if your dad didn't have a metal hip, he'd still be dancing, too." She lowered her hand. He saw behind her she had twisted some tinsel around the bookshelf. "Is this about the girl who stayed in your room?"

Adam looked at her.

"It's okay, Adam," she said. "Really. It's okay."

He wanted to pound something, to shake the steel frame of the chair until his mother rattled, wrap the tinsel around her neck. When Joe had cheated on Randall the first time, it had been so terrible Randall had gone to the other side of the world; the second time he had broken into four dry sticks and moved into their loft to die. Adam had been so angry with Joe he couldn't speak his name, and Randall would tell him, *You're only ten years old. You don't know yet what men do with their grief.* But he did know. He remembered how close Randall would hold him when he climbed into the metal bed; they'd be waiting for his mother or father to get home, and Randall would have one arm out of the sheets to write invisible words in the air, their names, Adam's address, various messages: *I'll love you forever,* and Adam had poked his finger into the air to write back to him in the cursive script he had just learned, *I love you, too.*

He put some music on in his room, loud, first some Hendrix, "Purple Haze," then some Sam Leavitt music, which was both electronic and magical in the style of the eighties. The beautiful noise saturated the room; the plaster and the glass, the furniture, even his body soaked and swelled with it. It was the music to *X,* Joe's last ballet for his father. The dance had been full of airy, swooping motions, none of the dirgelike stuff Joe had been obsessed with at the time. He would die in a year, but for Frankie, Joe had docked the funeral barge. Joe had hoped his dad and Sam would keep the company moored, but his dad and Sam couldn't keep anything moored. They kept commissioning vehicles for themselves; one by one the other dancers left the company. Even when his hip gave out and he had trouble negotiating the apartment, his father was unable to stop dancing. He took cortisone shots and spent four hours each afternoon at the chiropractor just so he could move on the stage at night for thirty-five minutes. Adam remembered the surge of the audience at his father's final performance, the way the crowd rose together in a crescendo to salute him. It was the last moment of his father's life.

Adam turned off the music. He understood now why Randall had journeyed to the stage just as Adam was basking in the heated applause, his made-up face lifted to the rafters. Randall had raised his hand to caution him, not to bless him.

～

Christmas morning, Adam said, "I'm going back to Princeton."

～

The campus was utterly, bleakly, empty and gray as he made his way from his car to his dorm room. It all felt so wrong he was half-afraid his key wouldn't work, but it did and now he sat at his desk with his bag and looked out the window thick with ice crystals. It was cold, but it had not snowed. Randall had lived in this same hall his sophomore year while he was studying art history. Adam had brought a few of Randall's art books with him to Princeton, and he picked up one of them now, the one with the big reproduction of *Departure* by Max Beckmann. The triptych was covered with notes on the boatman's stance and gaze, the purity of the sea, their destination, their wake, his relationships to the passengers he ferried, a king, a nobleman, a queen, and, on the queen's lap, a boy, a small, awkwardly drawn figure. Joe had not used the child for his ballet. But the boy was there.

Adam took the scissors from his desk drawer and, using the window as a mirror, began to hack at his ponytail. The blond cords of it thatched the floor, the chair, the desk, the pages of the book. When he was done, Adam put his face down into the painting, and his breath sent the hair skimming across the blue water. The sea was warm and calm and suffused with light, and beneath him he felt the oar hit the water.

A Midsummer
Night's Dream

Frederick Ashton
1904–1988

August 19, 1988

I've not slept the night since I turned eighty. I wake, always, at 4:00 A.M. All souls' hour. The room is full of odd shapes ... that pile on the chair a dwarf, a black mist by the panel, the bedpost a girl's curved neck.

I was given the Order of Merit by the queen, you know, November ten years ago, for having brought English ballet to its pinnacle. The ceremony stood in the Chapel Royal, St. James's Palace. There's a fixed galaxy of us meritocrats here on earth, only twenty-four persons. It won't be until I'm in God's galaxy that the queen can add another star to her own, though I don't suppose that impresses, with *your* view. So who's really up there? Who *are* the immortals? Michelangelo. Shakespeare. Tchaikovsky, I suppose. And Petipa? Definitely Petipa. He's the grand old man, after all. Lived in Russia practically his whole life, master of the czar's Imperial Ballet, ruler of the Maryinsky Theatre, and never learned a word of Russian. Did you know? Of course. He was

French. Ah well, French is the language of the dance. He owned *that* vocabulary. Every ballet that matters in the classical reper-tory is his: *Sleeping Beauty, Raymonda, Le Corsaire, La Bayadère, Don Quixote, Swan Lake.* And the staging. Four acts, every time, the full corps de ballet, the soloists, the demi-principals, the lead-ing dancers. He was a master of the crescendo, of exits and en-trances, of the grand pas de deux. He was Atlas, *is* Atlas, and he carries the ballet world on his shoulders, still.

And Pavlova? Certainly there. I saw her in Lima, in 1917, and it was, quite literally, the beginning of my life. Perhaps you could say, through her I *found* my life, though it would be another seven years before I'd attend my first ballet class. There were no dancers in my family, among people of my background. My fa-ther was vice-consul at the British embassy. One *went* to the bal-let; one was not *in* the ballet. I was thirteen when I saw Anna Pavlova do her signature *Dying Swan,* with her boneless arms and those velvet feet. I held my breath till the end of it, when she low-ered herself to the floor and bent her body over the one extended leg. That thick tutu with its feathers was splayed about her, and her head was hidden, bowed to her knee, the arms crossed over the ankle, and then, at the very last notes of the music, the foot be-spoke a final tremor. It was magic, I tell you. I've spent seventy *years* trying to re-create what she did with her arms and with her eyes. She was vibrance, a flame, not human at all. But she *was* human. At the soirees in her honor that month in Lima, I had trouble reconciling the woman I saw there, rather aged and beaked-nosed, with the spirit on that stage. Did you know, at one of those tango parties she saw my brother Tony dance, all whip-ping legs and bucking pelvis, and asked him to join her company on the spot? Not that he considered it for an instant. Yet, when I auditioned for her, years later, she turned *me* down flat!

I was never much of a dancer, truth be told. Will that count against me? I was already twenty when I had the money of my own to take my first class and such a naïf I wore cricket flannels into the studio. Leonid Massine had set up shop in London. He'd run away from Diaghilev and the Ballets Russes. Ballet was all Russian then, and the Ballets Russes was all the rage. To be English was to be an arriviste. To get out from under the Russian ballet, to make an *English* ballet, was always my mission. But the shadow of Mother Russia was so *huge.* One couldn't help but imitate. For years I made ballets about poor flower sellers and horny nymphs, all shades of the weakest work done at the Maryinsky. It changed for me, though, with *Symphonic Variations.* It was ballet blanc, in the genre of Petipa, grand and classical, but renewed. Take note. Yes, in 1946 I *invented* English ballet.

I met Serge Diaghilev in London in 1928, black suited, all imperial airs, his secretary a step behind. Very much the impresario. Scared me to death. He wasn't much impressed with me, I'm afraid. He found me plain. I was never *plain,* but I was no Nijinsky, if that was the standard. Diaghilev adored Nijinsky, that beautiful boy with his sloe eyes and calves shaped like diamonds. An immortal, hanging on a star as we speak, I'm sure. Why, the boy hung in the air down *here* when he jumped. Serge was obsessed with Nijinsky, and not only as a dancer. He fell in love with all his beautiful boys—Nijinsky, Massine, Dolin, Lifar. Just like Balanchine with the girls he'd marry and divorce, marry and divorce—when he could. What a fool he made of himself over that young Suzanne Farrell. Why, he threw her out of the company because she wouldn't fuck him. Can you imagine? Over the years I've done *my* yearning, but I'd never destroy my work over a fuck. No, I just put the boys into my ballets, a hundred ballets, a hundred bedtime stories: *Two Pigeons, A Month in the Country.* I won't tell you who each was for.

There's no fidelity in the queer world, you know, no sexual fidelity anyway. Everybody wants a young boy, a young body. Even I. But I was never vulgar about it, not like Nureyev with his bars or the hustlers he'd bring right to table with the queen, not that he was ever invited to table *there.* One must be discreet. I've always kept a clean slate. But then look where I came from. Nureyev, for all his airs, was the son of an army officer, and *he* was the son of a peasant. My equal, perhaps, in the theater, but you wouldn't find me at fifty out cruising the public parks. One must have some dignity. Why, if young Apollo came to me now, I'd give him a drink and send him away. Not that Apollo would come see me now. Why *is* it youth flees from age? And they flee from me, they flee from me. At the end of it, you're just an old queer, paying some woman to look after you.

It's 4:30. Where *is* Mrs. Dade?

Thank God, I had the fortune to become a choreographer. One doesn't have to look in the mirror at oneself each day to measure the decay. Most dancers retire at forty, and very few dancers last

216

that long—the whole thing is a race against debilitation. Margot was the exception; she was still strapping on those pointe shoes at age sixty-four, but she had to go on—what with Tito and all the bills. We'd had a pact that I would tell her when she'd had enough, but of course, when the time came, I couldn't speak a word. Yes, there have been only a few who danced until they died, and they all died young, except for Margot—Pavlova, Duncan, now Nureyev. All dead by fifty. At the end of his life, poor Nijinsky would write in his journals, "I am the clown of God." It's God's great joke, isn't it, that dancers outlive their bodies, outlive themselves.

But we need them young, need their young bodies. I did great work for Nureyev at his height, but Margot was my primary muse. I worked with her for *years* before Nureyev came on the scene and stole her away. The alacrity with which she embraced him! She was forty-two, almost ready to retire, and suddenly it was as if Michelangelo's finger of God reached out and touched her. There was nothing I could teach *him,* of course: he had trained at the Kirov, but by the time Nureyev defected, in '61, we English had something to offer—a living choreographer or two. The Soviet Union is dead to dance, has been the whole twentieth century. All the talent fled to Europe and to England, before the gates closed. And the ones trapped behind did the old warhorses or those terrible Communist ballets, *The Red Poppy,* or some such. No wonder they all started defecting like crazy. Ballet was moving forward without them. Why, in 1961 we were the Royal Ballet already, at Covent Garden. I worked up a grand thing to "Poème Tragique" to launch Nureyev in London. He was barechested, with a scarlet cloak covering him at the first. Oh, it made quite an impact; they screamed for him as if he were a matinee idol. He told me afterward I'd made him a bad dance, too gaudy, too many ingredients. Can you imagine? That Tatar temperament. He could be a bear, would tell Margot straight out in rehearsals, "You dance like shit." She would take it, but I gave back as good as I got. I didn't *care* for him, but I *used* him, and I have to say, I did *Marguerite and Armand* as much for him as for her, his Russian ardor, her English submission. Oh, you don't have to tell me. Margot and Rudi were too good to be lost to time.

And what of the ones who gave and gave and aren't remembered at all? For them, Death is the Gulag: absolute obliteration.

I need a drink. Can you imagine, I never liked the martini until my seventies.

Have I mentioned I do a bang-up impersonation of Isadora Duncan, her headless run, we called it, barefoot across the stage, back arched, arms behind her, head so tipped as to be invisible. Don't ask me to do it now. What a getup she always wore—she was forty-four by the time I saw her first, in one of those damned tunics. She was too heavy by then, but she could still reach down off the stage and grip one by the throat. She had one number to Chopin's "Funeral March" where she simply stood there in a cloak, head bowed, for *minutes,* until she opened the fabric to reveal her fat arms stuffed with lilies. That was theater—that was stasis made into dance. I used what I saw then later, that stasis, in *Symphonic Variations,* the cloak for Nureyev in *Poème Tragique,*

used the rest of what I remembered when I did my homage to Isadora. I plundered everything.

Does that make me less of an artist? We all plundered. Balanchine stole wholesale from Petipa. He shook with fear when his company toured Russia, lest the audience there recognize it. It's what you do with it. Balanchine took Petipa and made American dance—slicing extensions, gymnastic footwork, exaggerated arms; and I plundered to make English—emphasis on purity in épaulement, the line of the leg, delicacy in allegro. I moved on after *Symphonic Variations,* but Balanchine was mired in that sort of thing, plotless, characterless movement, always with the practice clothes and the blue cyclorama. All art to me is about stories, and my ballets had to have stories, costumes, characters and plots, *Cinderella, La Fille mal Gardée.* Tamara Karsavina, one of the czar's last great ballerinas, pressed me to do *Fille.* She sat down with me, though she was *my* age *now,* and recalled for me entire the ballet's libretto, bit by bit, right down to the ribbon dance, the *pas de ruban.* Oh, it was glorious—the big pink roll of it stretching across the stage. It was used for the first time in the production Karsavina danced at the Maryinsky, and I loved the full circle of it, Russian ballet remade English style. Balanchine wanted to break with Petipa's heritage; I wanted not to break with him but to *extend* him. I have to say, I don't know where *you* rank him, but I always found Balanchine's work very dry. For his part, he always thought me an old Turkish lady, reclining on the divan, sucking at my hookah. He told me once what he'd learned from me—to pile up the dinner dishes in the sink and run water over them before the charwoman arrives. Yes, that was the totality of what I had to offer him. Well, I didn't have *his* start at the Maryinsky school, and, no, all the Russian fairies weren't gathered at *my* christening, but still I met him at the summit. This century had Balanchine and me. I scan the horizon now and I see nobody. Who will bring us along?

But I never had an *interest* in students or administration, the girls in one's office, weeping and complaining. Remiss of me? Ninette did all that, Ninette de Valois, why the woman had to bend my arm to make me take over the directorship in 1963. It was her company to start with, I was the hired hand, brought along in 1930 to give the boys and girls something to dance. We were just the Vic-Wells back then, later Sadler's Wells, only *finally* the Royal Ballet in all its grandeur. Balanchine conceived his entire project like Athena born whole, not willy-nilly: school, company, theater. He had energy, but even the grandest energy winds down to nothing eventually. Balanchine spent a year lingering in that hospital, and all the while idling in his mind's eye were pretty people doing pretty things he could do nothing about. His ballets are performed in theaters all over the world now, you know. He's in his grave five years, but there are bits of him everywhere, like a sparkler gone off, like an inverted heaven, like heaven on earth.

Ah, yes, I see.

When it gets light, I'll sit out in the topiary garden on my bench with my cigs and my Chinese checkers. Where are my teeth? Oh, bugger old age.

Why, it's gotten to the point I'll turn *down* invitations to dinner: one cannot hawk up phlegm before the Queen Mother, bent over the garbage pail, holding one's teeth in the air. I met the queen through her daughter, Margaret. The princess was mad about the ballet, always had me slip her into rehearsal when Fonteyn and Nureyev were in the studio. That's how I entertained: I had people into the studio. At home, I simply hadn't the proper milieu, just old Mrs. Dade, who certainly isn't up to the Snowdons or the Queen Mother. No. I'm a guest. I go to Sternfield or Sandringham, where we play charades, dance ballets in the pool, drink strong martinis till supper. Little Freddie Ashton from Lima, Peru, two fingers from the beau monde. *They* understood who I was. I've mentioned I received the Order of Merit? That I'm Sir Frederick Ashton, OM? Ninette was a propmaster. *I* made the Royal Ballet *royal*. *I* was the season. *I* was English dance.

Yes, it *has* been a long time since I've been in the studio. It was *only* two years past, I think, with that young American dancer, Sandra Ellis, who'd been making a sensation with their Ballet Theatre. She was thin as a reed and so high-strung she had to bring her husband with her to every class and rehearsal. He's the mule in her stable, I suppose. The poor chap has to sit there, can't even look in a book, loaded up with her woollies and shoes, bags full of her props everywhere. Looked like a spaniel—no, too small, more like a sheepdog, or better, a basset, with the thermos of whiskey. It's in the training now: the girls are pressed so hard, the competition so stiff, they crack. At sixteen, Margot was nothing compared with these girls, with that bulb on her nose and her sloppy feet: she'd not be taken into any company in the world today in that state. In the old days, our girls had figures, and lives.

They had time. The boys suffer, too—look at Godunov leaning on the crutch of his vodka, or that beautiful Robbie Perez, dead at twenty-seven from an overdose. They all wear such beautiful shells, one misses the decay from within. This Sandra Ellis did *Sleeping Beauty* at Covent Garden, and that presence, that fragility: it was magic. On the stage, she's perfection; in the flesh, well, brown circles beneath the eyes, and bones, all I could see were bones. Whatever idea I had wanted to do on her fled me like a refugee. I was desperate. I paged through the score, finally switched music altogether—it happens, it happens. It doesn't mean I'm finished. The Muse is not always at the ready.

And what of my more than a half century in the theater? What of *Symphonic Variations, Ondine,* my *Sleeping Beauty, A Midsummer Night's Dream*? What of all my ballets? Don't any of them count? *You* tell *me*.

Margot? No, no, it's not Margot. She's in Panama, ill to the bone.

I hear she wants to be cremated, ashes buried atop Tito's grave. What an appalling marriage, yet she clings to it. Not that I begrudged her the money. Lord, no, I *hate* the idea of dancers living on potatoes once their careers are over, they get no pensions at all, you know, not even Margot, after all those years. But Tito never treated her well, not until he was shot; then, of course, he depended on her utterly. He simply never respected her as a woman, and he never respected her as an artist. If she was dancing a part he liked, he'd come to the theater just for his favorite bit—she'd tell him to arrive at 9:12 or some such, down to the minute. And that pomaded hair and unctuous Latin charm. But Margot needed him, needed to be Mrs. Roberto Arias, wife of the Panamanian ambassador to Britain. She was lost offstage, you know. As are we all.

~≈

Surely there must be some compensation in the next world for the loneliness in this one. I've lived as long as the century, and I can count on one hand the years I've been loved.

~≈

I think Nureyev was actually happy to find he'd die young. It was too painful for him to stop dancing, though he had lost almost everything that had made him great as a dancer. So now his great mystery lies before him and he knows the *how,* if not the *when.* It's always been the *way* one would go, not the *going* that bothers me, anyway. Oh, I've dreaded the notion of keeling over in the street with a heart attack, the way poor Pushkin did in Leningrad. One's face in the pavement. The indignity. Can you imagine? No. I never wanted to die in a public place, nor linger in a private one. Still. Still.

~≈

Every now and again, you know, something stirs. There's a piece of music that draws me. Not a long ballet, mind you. But a half hour perhaps. After all, Petipa was my age when he started his masterpiece. It was *Swan Lake.* The stamina he must have had. Four acts, of course. He must have begun it in summer, like this. It's a summer ballet, the lush lake, the swans, the heavy perfume of sorcery. Odette, the princess trapped inside those white

223

feathers; Siegfried, the prince on his Germanic country estate charged with breaking the enchantment. When he fails, he breaks it anyway, leaping with her to their deaths. People think the ballet is about love, but Petipa was seventy-six when he created it, and I'll tell you, *that* ballet is about only one thing: Death. Petipa has Odette and Siegfried sail beyond Death's reach, at rest on the golden boat of Art, suspended above Oblivion. Yes, it is a terror, to be forgotten. Petipa asked the question in 1895, almost a hundred years ago. Well, he has *his* answer. Why, just look at *Swan Lake*. The work lives. It lives, and it will be done until kingdom come.

Every stage is haunted. One can feel the ghosts clustering about, begging to be remembered, a mist of feathers, resin, and paint.

Pavlova called for her Swan costume when she lay dying of pneumonia, had it laid across her body, bodice to breast. What shall I ask for, now that your head's on *my* pillow? Grandeur then, if not immortality. All the grandeur *this* world has to offer. I want my service held at Westminster Abbey. Yes, it's the Abbey or nothing.

Ah, your breath, I can see it, I see it blowing the ribbons across the ceiling, the pink color unrolling, so beautiful, so fey. And the patterns—the ribbons from *Fille mal Gardée*! Oh—watch out there—this one goes under, girls, look out for the loop! Cat's cradle now, hold it and—careful—uncross and into the spokes of the cartwheel. Pull on that end, tightly now. Keep running, girls! Keep running! Look at the colors. My God, it's dawn, isn't it, it's the colors of dawn.

A Note on the Sources

I depended for information on a number of sources. For "Don Quixote," I relied upon Bernard Taper's *Balanchine: A Biography*, Richard Buckle's *George Balanchine: Ballet Master*, Robert Garis's *Following Balachine*, Allegra Kent's *Once a Dancer*, and Suzanne Farrell's *Holding onto the Air*. Articles by David Daniel in *Vanity Fair* in 1987, and by Holly Brubach in *The New York Times Magazine* and Robert Gottlieb in *Vanity Fair* in 1998 were also essential. For "A Short Season," Barbara Arias's *Misha: The Mikhail Baryshnikov Story*, articles by John Gruen in *Dance Magazine* in 1982, by Jennifer Dunning in *The New York Times* and Shelley Levitt in *People* magazine in 1995, and by Joan Acocella in *The New Yorker* in 1998, as well as the documentary *Godunov: The World to Dance In* were particularly helpful. For "The Immortals," I drew upon three wonderful biographies: Otis Stuart's *Perpetual Motion: The Public and Private Lives of Rudolf Nureyev*, Diane Solway's *Nureyev: His Life*, and Julie Kavanagh's *Secret Muses*, as well as Alexander Bland's books *Fonteyn and Nureyev* and *The Nureyev Image*. And finally, for "A Midsummer Night's Dream," Kavanagh's *Secret Muses* was again an essential source.

White Swan,
Black Swan

ADRIENNE SHARP

A Reader's Guide

A Conversation with Adrienne Sharp

Raiford Rogers, a Los Angeles–based choreographer, is the director of both the Los Angeles Chamber Ballet and the Raiford Rogers Modern Ballet, as well as choreographer in residence at the Los Angeles County Museum of Art. His work has been performed throughout the U.S., Europe, and Latin America. The recipient of two National Endowment for the Arts choreographer fellowships, Mr. Rogers serves on numerous arts panels, most recently as a judge for the Alberto Vilar Global Fellowships. He also directs and hosts Artshift, which profiles leading Los Angeles artists and architects and airs as part of Life & Times on KCET PBS.

Raiford Rogers: You were a trainee for Harkness Ballet in New York City. What was the path that brought you there?

Adrienne Sharp: Like most little girls, I entered the ballet world at the age of seven, but unlike most little girls, I didn't leave that world until I was eighteen and a trainee at Harkness. Looking back on it now, I see that all the little schools— the Miss Debbie's and Miss Linda's, and in my case, Miss Ellen's—are just trolling grounds for talent. A dancer's life is very short, and the ranks must be constantly replenished, and so all these teachers are on the lookout for talent. If you have the right body type and show a facility for movement, you are going to find your training encouraged and intensified. Which happened to me. By the time I was ten years old, I was on full scholarship and taking ballet class six days a week, and when I wasn't dancing I was going to the ballet and reading *Dance Magazine* and collecting souvenir programs from all the leading ballet companies. I could still tell you the names of all the corps de ballet, soloists, and principal dancers from American Ballet Theater, New York City Ballet, and the Royal Ballet during the sixties and seventies. I'd cut out the pictures of these dancers and paste them together onto poster board, and then I'd take a black magic marker and scrawl across the collage "Dance Is Life for Those of Us Who Choose It." I was obsessed. By the time I was fifteen, I barely attended high school at all, and by the time I was seventeen, I was living on my own in New York and studying on full scholarship at Harkness.

RR: What was that like?

AS: Very magical and very humbling. I was called a trainee, but the company had disintegrated a few months before I arrived there. Photographs of the dancers were still all over the walls, and the school—with a faculty that included Renita Exter and David Howard—was still going strong. Rebecca Harkness had turned her East Seventies townhouse into the school, and I took class in beautifully equipped studios with chandeliers hanging from the ceilings. Unfortunately, I was miserable in class, where I slumped at the barre, no longer the star pupil. Every scholarship class in New York is filled with girls who were the stars at their local schools, and only some of these girls will go on to dance professionally, filling the small number of spots open in American and European companies. I wasn't one of them. I came home after several months and threw myself on my bed with no idea what to do next. My parents held nervous, worried conferences outside my bedroom door because they, too, had no idea what I would do next. All I had ever done was dance.

RR: What did you do next?

AS: Eventually I went to college and discovered writing. But I was lucky to be admitted to college at all, since education—any class that didn't have to do with dancing—was of no interest to me up until that time. All dance students struggle to combine high school academics and dance training. If you're going to be taken into a company at the age of sixteen, seventeen, or eighteen, your most intensive training is going to be done during your high school years. Many dancers give up on high school. In her autobiography Suzanne Farrell writes of struggling through an algebra test in the morning and running in late to a rehearsal with Balanchine and Stravinsky. Finally she told her mother she just couldn't do both anymore. I spoke recently with a young dancer in New York City Ballet, who at age twenty finally got her high school diploma, and she managed that only because she was sidelined with a foot injury for a year.

RR: So you went to college and discovered writing. When did you start writing about dancers?

AS: For a long while I wrote the usual stories about twenty-somethings in love. And then one day I made one of the characters in one of my stories a dancer, and I showed this story to Peter Taylor. I was a Hoyns Fellow at The University of Virginia at that time, and I can still recall him sitting in his office, winter, floor heater glowing, Persian carpet, Peter Taylor at his desk, his hair a pure white. He told me I needed to figure out what it was I wanted to say about this world, this ballet world, what were its larger issues and themes. I was twenty-five at the time and I left his office thinking, "I don't know anything about larger issues and themes," and I put the story aside. A few years later, I returned to it, and whether it was maturity or distance from that part of my life, I don't know, but suddenly I knew what I wanted to say. I began to write seriously about dancers, and it was as if the two halves of my life came together.

For a long while I had thought that all the time I'd spent dancing was wasted time, but I now discovered that none of it was wasted. All the useless details I knew so well—breaking in pointe shoes, weeping in the dressing room, dancing in recitals, desperate dieting before weigh-in—I could now use to create a sense of verisimilitude for the stories. And I discovered something else as I began to write about dancing. Almost all the fiction set in the dance world is written for children, even though this world offers so many adult issues to explore.

RR: What are some of those issues?

AS: For one, every dancer's life is a race against age and debilitation. A dancer has a very short season in which to perfect her craft and display it on the stage before injury or time overtakes her. Most dancers leave dancing somewhere in their twenties. Only the soloists and principal dancers last longer, and they find themselves with fewer and fewer peers. The greatest dancers retire in their early forties, and there are only a teaspoon of dancers of that age in each company. I imagine it's increasingly lonely at the top.

We know every dancer is exceptionally ambitious and driven. What happens when that ambition is frustrated? Alexander Godunov is a famous case in point, but there are frustrated dancers in every company in the world. Sexual politics have always played a part in ballet, to the dismay of many dancers in the Tsar's Imperial Ballet, in Diaghilev's Ballet Russes, and in Balanchine's New York City Ballet. What does romantic obsession do to the lover and to the beloved? AIDS decimated the ranks of ballet companies and stole the life of Rudolf Nureyev. The illness is grievous, and it destroys the very instrument of the art. I was interested also in what makes genius flourish and at what cost to the family and friends who surround him. All of these are issues at stake in the stories.

RR: Some of the stories are biographical fictions, of Balanchine, Fonteyn and Nureyev, Godunov, Ashton. These figures have been the subjects of straight biographies. What were you hoping to do with them as fiction?

AS: I was hoping to tell their stories to a wider audience, to readers who might not pick up an eight hundred page biography of Nureyev and who might not be balletomanes, but who would like to look through a window into that world for a while and have it presented in story, with the accompanying, satisfying structure of rising action, climax, and denouement. The most difficult aspect for me in writing these stories was in finding that dramatic arc to set events along. What part of the life or what theme in the life lends itself to a story? I couldn't simply retell the life; I had to dramatize a portion of it. For the story about Balanchine, I explored his need for a muse, for a body on which to create, without which he was paralyzed. And I played the ideas of movement and paralysis against each other as Balanchine moved from his wife—the beautiful Tanaquil LeClerq, paralyzed by polio at the height of her career—to the young Suzanne Farrell, who danced every night season after season. She was nothing but body and movement. When Farrell left City Ballet, Balanchine was so depressed that he was unable to create for several years. For the Godunov story, the dramatic crux was his rivalry with Mikhail Baryshnikov, which began when they were children together, studying ballet in Riga. The story about Fonteyn and Nureyev pitted their onstage love affair against their offstage story. The Ashton piece was a chance for reflection both on the lives of the other dancers in the book and on his own life, which spanned the big ballet century from Diaghilev and the diaspora of all those dancers to New York, Paris, and London, where they formed or invigorated the great ballet companies those cities host today. And, of course, fiction does what biography can't, which is to speak, see, and feel right from the center of the subject.

RR: Can you talk a little about the title, <u>White Swan, Black Swan</u>. It refers, of course, to <u>Swan Lake</u>, to Odette, the white swan and victim of von Rothbart's sorcery, and to Odile, the black swan and von Rothbart's partner in thwarting Odette's release from the spell. Were you drawing a parallel to the ballet?

AS: Mikhail Baryshnikov once said a dancer's life is a beautiful tragedy, and I think what he meant by this is that the art is a beautiful art and its practitioners are beauty personified, but a dancer's life is brief, so brief, and therein lies the tragedy. So a dancer's life is light and shadow. An artist can paint, a writer can write, an actor can act, a musician can play until the end of her life, but a dancer must retire in the prime of hers, or else risk the humiliation of slowly deteriorating in public. Rudolf Nureyev was actually booed when he appeared on the stage of the Paris Opera at the end of his career, and he danced longer than he should have, driven by some instinct that dancing would help him to fight his illness. Gwen Verdon said that every dancer dies two deaths. That's how a dancer views retirement: death.

RR: Dancing does cast a spell, and not just on professional dancers. What is the draw?

AS: I think it's not only the beauty of the art that draws us, but also the discipline and rigor of it. You devote yourself to the barre and to the ideal of perfection, and everything else falls away. That was my experience, an utter single-mindedness that becomes the center of your life. Which is why so many dancers and serious dance students have enormous trouble readjusting to the outside world.

Serious ballet study begins when children are at an enormously impressionable age. If you study long enough, you'll be haunted by it forever. There's all the worship of the older students and their beauty and perfection. I remember sitting under the big piano at Washington School of Ballet, watching the fabulous Mary Day coaching Kevin McKenzie (now the director of American Ballet Theater) and his partner Suzanne Longley for the International Ballet Competition at Varna, where they took silver and bronze medals. Talk about idol worship. I trembled when Suzanne spoke to me, spent hours trying to do my hair just the way she did hers.

RR: Some of your readership is made up of dance students and balletomanes, and they already know the stories of the ballets and the ballet vocabulary. How do you make your work accessible to those without such knowledge?

AS: Some quick exposition delineates the stories of the ballets, or the essential elements of them. In describing the actual dancing, I forego a lot of formal vocabulary and describe an attitude as an "impossible, backwards C" or a developpe front as "My leg is extended high and pressed between us like a sword." Anyone can visualize these movements, and of course the language carries a connotation: the girl dancing in this story is in a difficult, impossible personal relationship, which she is about to sever. The stories are always about characters; the dancing I describe has to move the story forward dramatically.

RR: What are you working on now? Will your next book be about dancers?

AS: I'm writing a novel set in New York in 1981–83, Balanchine's last years. He'd had a long-time dream to produce a full-length *Sleeping Beauty*, the ballet he fell in love with when he was ten years old, standing in the wings of the Maryinsky Theater. He was a student at the Imperial Ballet school, and children from the school were performing that night in the ballet, as cupids or little monsters in the Carabosse's train, or as flower-bearing dancers in the Garland Waltze. What Balanchine saw on the stage that night set the course for his life. In my novel I give him a chance to re-create the ballet, though in fact he was too sick to actually do it, and we follow his influence over the young girl he casts as Aurora. She is, in effect, his last muse, with all the benefits and costs of such a position.

Reading Group Questions and Topics for Discussion

1. The stories explore many different stages of a dancer's life—the ballet student in "The Brahmins," the fledgling corps de ballet dancer in "Wili," the ballet stars in "Bugaku" and "The Immortals," the aging choreographers in "Don Quixote" and "A Midsummer Night's Dream." How do the characters at each stage feel about their endeavors?

2. Many of the titles of the stories refer to characters in a ballet or to the titles of a ballet—*Giselle*, *Swan Lake*, *Bugaku*, *Sleeping Beauty*, *La Bayadère*, *A Midsummer Night's Dream*. In what ways do the characters and stories of these ballets reflect the action and characters of the book?

3. *White Swan, Black Swan* mixes together real life ballet figures, such as Alexander Godunov, Margot Fonteyn, and George Balanchine, with entirely fictional creations. In what way is the book enriched by this juxtaposition?

4. American Ballet Theater ballet mistress Elena Tchernichova observed that many dancers come from unhappy homes. In the stories "In the Wake" and "In the Kingdom of the Shades," both young dancer protagonists have problems with their parents. In "Prince of Desire" and "White Swan, Black Swan," the main characters struggle with disintegrating marriages. In what ways do these personal problems affect them professionally?

5. Many of the dancers in the book must deal with the gap between the perfection they seek and their frustration with the

level of accomplishment they are actually able to achieve. How do these dancers come to terms with their despair?

6. Many of the stories are interrelated, in that we see a character first in one story and then in another. How has Adam grown and changed from "Departure" to "Ax"? In what way has Joanna's obsession with ballet in "Bugaku" both frightened and inspired her brother in "Prince of Desire"? Why does Kate quit ballet in "Wili" only to return to it at the end of "The Brahmins"? What has Robbie Perez destroyed in the women he loves in "White Swan, Black Swan" and "In the Kingdom of the Shades"?

7. The book opens with the story "Bugaku" and closes with the reminiscences of Frederick Ashton in "A Midsummer Night's Dream." Why does "Bugaku" open the collection and why does "A Midsummer Night's Dream" close it?

8. The title of the book, *White Swan, Black Swan*, refers to both the beauty and the difficulty of a dancer's life. What beauty do you see throughout the book? What darkness?

© David LaPorte

About the Author

ADRIENNE SHARP studied ballet from the age of seven and trained with the prestigious Harkness Ballet in New York. She received an M.A. with honors from The Writing Seminars at The Johns Hopkins University and was awarded a Henry Hoyns Fellowship in fiction at the University of Virginia. Her short stories have appeared in *Redbook*, the *Northwest Review*, and other literary quarterlies. She lives in Los Angeles with her husband and two children.